Mallory Pike, #1 Fan

**Other books by
Ann M. Martin**

Rachel Parker, Kindergarten Show-off
Eleven Kids, One Summer
Ma and Pa Dracula
Yours Turly, Shirley
Ten Kids, No Pets
Slam Book
Just a Summer Romance
Missing Since Monday
With You and Without You
Me and Katie (the Pest)
Stage Fright
Inside Out
Bummer Summer

BABY-SITTERS LITTLE SISTER series
THE BABY-SITTERS CLUB mysteries
THE BABY-SITTERS CLUB series

Mallory Pike, #1 Fan
Ann M. Martin

AN
APPLE
PAPERBACK

SCHOLASTIC INC.
New York Toronto London Auckland Sydney

To Summer Lynne Headley

The author gratefully acknowledges
Suzanne Weyn
for her help in
preparing this manuscript.

ISBN 0-590-48224-6

Copyright © 1994 by Ann M. Martin. All rights reserved. Published by Scholastic Inc. THE BABY-SITTERS CLUB ® and APPLE PAPERBACKS ® are registered trademarks of Scholastic Inc.

12 11 10 9 8 7 6 5 4 3 2 1   4 5 6 7 8 9/9

Printed in the U.S.A.   40

First Scholastic printing, November 1994

CHAPTER 1

I love English class. I really do. And today I was loving it more than ever. My teacher, Mr. Williams, was giving us this really interesting assignment. "I want you to think about a career you might be interested in pursuing someday," he told the class. "Then express something about that career in written form. It can be a series of poems, a report, a play, a short story. Be creative. I don't want a report *on* your prospective career. I want to know *why* it interests you. How does the career fit into your view of what matters in life? What is it about *you* that feels drawn to this career choice?"

My best friend, Jessi Ramsey, raised her hand. "You mean, we can do anything we want?" she asked when Mr. Williams called on her.

"Well, yes and no," replied Mr. Williams. "I'm giving you a lot of leeway, but I want to know what you're doing. By the end of next week each of you must submit a one-page written proposal telling me what you plan to do. After I've read your proposal I'll have a short conference with you. I'll either give you the go-ahead, or we'll discuss ways to shape the project further."

That sounded fair enough to me. One thing I love about Mr. Williams is that he treats us like adults. Not many teachers would give a sixth-grade class this much freedom.

Picking a career would be easy for me. I've always known what I want to be — an author of books for children.

I've loved reading and writing forever. When I was ten, I met one of my favorite authors, Amelia Moody, at a book signing in the Washington Mall. The meeting was sort of a disaster. (I got so nervous I burst into tears. Not *too* embarrassing!) But meeting her and seeing how much her work affected so many kids made me absolutely certain that I wanted to be an author, too.

The day I see the name Mallory Pike (that's me) on the cover of a book will be the greatest day of my life. I can easily imagine it. That may be because I spend a *lot* of time imagining it.

One thing I don't like to imagine, though, is my picture on the jacket flap. That's because

I can't stand the way I look. I don't have a monster face or anything, but I *do* have freckles, glasses, and a terrible nose. (I'm told I inherited my nose from my grandfather, who died before I was born. I wish I'd inherited a horse farm or a million dollars instead.) I also have curly reddish brown hair which does whatever it wants. Plus, I have braces. At least they're the clear kind, so no one calls me metal mouth or anything like that. Jessi always tells me I'm better looking than I think I am, but *I* think she's just being a pal. Maybe I'll forget the author picture and let kids imagine what I look like. Why spoil a good book for them?

"Your grade for this assignment will make up eighty percent of your grade this marking period, and you'll have the remainder of the marking period to complete the assignment," Mr. Williams continued. "So, give it some hard thought and come up with something that will really hold your interest."

I glanced at Jessi. Her chin was propped on her hands and her delicate, dark brows were knit into a thoughtful frown. She'd obviously started the hard thinking part already. Of course, I knew what her career choice would be. Jessi is a super-talented ballerina. She studies twice a week at a ballet school in Stamford, the city closest to Stoneybrook, Connecticut, where we live. Jessi has even danced in some

3

professional productions. So, like me, Jessi knew exactly what she wanted to do her project on. The tricky part would be working ballet into a written project. But knowing Jessi, she'd come up with something clever.

Meanwhile, I had absolutely no idea how I wanted to do my project. Writing something about being a writer seemed to offer endless possibilities. I *would* have to think hard. I could have a great time with this assignment if I came up with something good.

The bell rang for the end of second period. I gathered my books and joined Jessi. "What are you going to do for your project?" I asked her.

"Well, I was thinking that I could interview Madame Noelle about her life as a dancer." (Madame Noelle is Jessi's dance teacher.)

"Good idea. That would be like reporting on the history of ballet for the last hundred years," I teased. I've seen Mme. Noelle, and she's *old*.

Jessi smiled. "She's not *that* old. What are you going to do?"

We stepped out into the hallway and entered the flow of students changing class. "I have no idea. None," I admitted.

"You could write about winning that award for your short story," Jessi suggested. I'd won Best Overall Fiction in the Sixth Grade for my story, "Caught in the Middle," on Young Author's Day.

"What would I say about it?" I asked.

Jessi shrugged. "I don't know — how hard it was to write, and how you felt when you won?"

"No, I don't think that would be enough. I'll think of something, though." Which was exactly what I did for the rest of the day — think.

I was still thinking about the assignment when I walked through the front door of my house that afternoon. As usual, things were a little wild.

The triplets, who are ten, were each wrapped in one of my father's white dress shirts, and each one had a tie knotted around his head. They were pretending to be ninjas, slicing the air and jumping off the living room sofa yelling "Ha! Ya!" like a bunch of maniacs. Adam, Byron, and Jordan are identical, although I have no problem telling them apart. I knew which ninja was which.

My sister Vanessa paid no attention to the ninja triplets. She was busy trying to master one of those Skip-It rings. You know, those giant ankle rings, with a rope attached. You put one foot through the ring, and use that foot to swing the rope around, then you jump over the rope with the other foot. She wasn't having much luck. Like me, Vanessa is a dud at most sports. (She's a good writer, though. For a nine-year-old, she writes some pretty amazing poems.)

Nicky, who is eight, was driving our bassett hound Pow insane with his new Squiggle Ball. The ball has a battery inside and *never* quits moving. Even if it shoots under a dresser it will roll its way out. Pow was trying to catch it, but the ball never stopped, so he couldn't.

Margo (she's seven) was trying to get Claire (she's four) to play Skatch. Even with the Velcro mitt, which the Velcro ball sticks to, Claire couldn't catch it (another female Pike athletic superstar in the making).

Sometimes the craziness of my house bugs me. But today I was too deep in thought. I dodged three flying ninjas, stepped over a Squiggle Ball and a bassett hound, ducked a runaway flash of wild pink Velcro, and hopped over a Skip-It rope, barely noticing any of it as I made my way across the living room. I just had to come up with a good project.

I was halfway up the stairs when I heard the phone ring. "Vanessa," Mom called my sister from the kitchen. "Phone. It's Haley."

Haley Braddock is Vanessa's best friend. Hearing Haley's name gave me a thought. Haley is a member of a club in the Stoneybrook

Elementary School called the Kids-Can-Do-Anything Club. Jessi's younger sister, Becca, belongs to it, too. The members of the KCDAC, or Kids Club (as most members call it), do a lot of community service work, such as organize food drives and recycling projects. I wondered if I could find a way to include the club members in my English project. After all, my future career would involve writing for kids, so shouldn't kids be a part of the project? It seemed like a natural connection.

But how could I include them?

By the time I reached the room I share with Vanessa, I had that limp, brain-drain feeling you get from thinking about one thing for too long. I decided to put the project aside for awhile. Instead, I took a novel called *Alice Anderson* from my backpack. I'd checked it out from the Stoneybrook Middle School library. (SMS is my school.)

Alice Anderson, the main character, is a seventeen-year-old girl who lives in a small farming town. She is the only girl in a family of four brothers. Alice dreams of going to Hollywood and becoming a movie star but she has no idea how she'll make it out of her small town, because her family is poor.

I had taken *Alice Anderson* from the library because I needed to do a book report. It looked interesting, but I never expected it to be so hysterically funny. It doesn't sound like it would be, but it is. Alice's brothers are always getting in messes. When Alice tries to help them out, she ends up in worse trouble.

In the last chapter I had read, Alice's brothers want Alice to perform the lead role in the town play because they think some big talent scout is in the audience, so they lock the nasty lead actress in the closet. When Alice hears what they've done she goes wild trying to get the closet door open. She succeeds in setting the actress free, but accidentally knocks over the man who plays the back half of the mule. Alice is the only one who can fit the mule costume, so she takes his part, and makes her brother, Sven, put on the maid's costume and take her small part. Sven keeps forgetting the lines, so Alice whispers them to him from the back of the mule outfit, which makes everyone in the audience laugh.

Crazy things like that are always happening to Alice. But the cool thing about the book is the way her family sticks together. No matter what happens, Mrs. Anderson, the mother, always manages to make a big dinner and the family sits around laughing about whatever it was that went wrong.

I stretched out on my bed and opened *Alice Anderson*. In a second, I felt as if I were there with the Andersons. Henrietta Hayes, the author, had to be a genius. How could she think of so many funny things to write? Her characters were so happy and full of fun. Just reading the book gave me a great feeling.

When I reached the last pages, my eyes brimmed with tears. Nothing sad had happened. I was just touched by how Alice's brothers saved all their money to buy her a train ticket to Hollywood. And then Alice cashed it in so their youngest brother, Evan, could have an emergency operation. (He'd fallen through a weak spot in the ice while ice fishing to earn money for Alice's ticket.) In the end, Evan was all right, and the family sat around the big dinner table laughing and having a good time.

Maybe tears filled my eyes because the book was over. I hate when a good book ends.

One way I judge whether or not a book is great is if I feel I know the author when I'm done reading. If I do, then it was a great book! I definitely felt that I knew Henrietta Hayes. It was as if we were friends. I wanted to tell her how much I loved her book, just the way you'd tell a friend who'd written something great.

I wiped my eyes and took a sheet of my good stationery from my top dresser drawer. In my best handwriting, I began a letter to Henrietta Hayes.

Dear Ms. Hayes,

I have just finished reading Alice Anderson. It's one of the best books I've ever read. I hope you've written other books because I'd like to read them all.

When did you write your first book? How did you get your ideas for Alice Anderson? Is Alice Anderson you? Did you want to be an actress before becoming a writer? Did you really have such funny brothers? Or, are you the Mrs. Anderson character? Well, thanks for writing such a great book. I hope you can answer this letter if you have the time.

Sincerely,
Mallory Pike, a new fan

I opened to the title page of the book, and turned it over. The address of the publishing company was printed there. (It's there in any book.) Publishing companies pass people's letters on to authors. I knew this because I'd once written to Amelia Moody.

After copying the address onto an envelope, I put the letter inside and sealed it. Mom usually has stamps, so I'd borrow one from her and drop the letter in the mailbox on the way to my BSC meeting.

Oh! I can't believe I haven't mentioned the BSC to you yet. It stands for Baby-sitters Club. Along with writing and books, it's one of the most important parts of my life. And at that very moment, I was dangerously close to being late for a meeting!

CHAPTER 2

Even though I'm no athlete, I slid into my BSC meeting like a baseball player sliding into home base. "Made it!" I cried, watching the digital clock in Claudia Kishi's bedroom change from 5:29 to 5:30.

Kristy Thomas, the club president, called the meeting to order. "That was awfully close," she said. Kristy is a fanatic about being on time. Every meeting must start at five-thirty — sharp! Five-thirty-one is not acceptable. (If you're late you get the dreaded Look from Kristy. You know that expression, if looks could kill? Well, her Look definitely could.)

"I was finishing a great book and I lost track of time," I explained. "But I'm here."

Before I go on, I should explain to you what the Baby-sitters Club is all about. We meet every Monday, Wednesday, and Friday afternoon from five-thirty until six o'clock. During that time parents who need reliable baby-sitting can call and reach a group of sitters all at once. One of us is bound to be free to take the job. It saves them a lot of calling. We're very popular with parents around here.

The BSC was Kristy's great idea. It came to her one day when her mother was trying to find a sitter for her younger brother, David Michael, and not having much luck. Kristy told her idea to her best friend, Mary Anne Spier. Then they told their friend Claudia. Claudia told her new friend Stacey McGill, and the BSC was born. They put up some fliers around Stoneybrook and, almost instantly, the club was successful.

Business grew so much that they added another member, Dawn Schafer, who had recently moved to Stoneybrook from California. Five sitters worked fine, but after awhile Stacey had to move away. (Although she eventually came back, at the time we thought Stacey was gone forever.) That's when Jessi and I were invited to join. We're junior officers since we're eleven and the others are all thirteen. We baby-sit only on weekends or during afternoons (unless we're sitting for our own siblings), but that frees other members to take more evening jobs, so it works out well.

Recently, we've had another staff switch. Dawn went back to California to stay for awhile with her father and brother. (Her parents are divorced.) In her absence, Shannon Kilbourne is filling in. Before Dawn left, Shannon was an associate member, which meant she didn't come to meetings regularly. Instead, we'd call her up when we needed her to take sitting jobs no one else was free for. Now, she attends meetings.

Let me tell you about the members of the club. I'll start with Jessi, since you already know a little about her. As I've said, she's a talented ballerina and my very best friend. Like me, she loves to read, especially books about horses. Unlike me, she doesn't have a huge family. Her family consists of her mother, father, her younger sister Becca, and her little brother Squirt (his real name is John Philip Ramsey, Jr.). Jessi's Aunt Cecelia lives with them, too. She takes care of Becca and Squirt while Mr. and Mrs. Ramsey are at work.

Jessi moved to Stoneybrook from Oakley, New Jersey. (She moved into Stacey's old house!) The move was difficult for the Ramseys. They are African-American, and their neighborhood back in New Jersey was comfortably integrated. Stoneybrook is mostly white, and some of the Ramseys' new neighbors weren't exactly happy about a black family moving in. Experiencing this kind of

14

prejudice was painful for Jessi's family. (When I think of people hurting Jessi's feelings like that, I get furious.) But the Ramseys waited it out, and now their neighbors know them as the nice people they are.

The best way to describe Jessi is to say she looks like a dancer. She's slim, with long legs, and she moves gracefully no matter what she's doing. She has big brown eyes with long lashes. Her dark hair is usually pulled back, dancer-style, in a ponytail or bun.

Next, I'll tell you about Kristy Thomas. I think of Kristy in terms of opposites. Here is Kristy opposite number one: small physical size, huge personality. She is a petite person, the shortest one of us. Yet she has a big presence. Kristy doesn't keep anything to herself. She lets you know exactly what she's thinking — and she's always thinking something. Great ideas are Kristy's trademark.

Kristy opposite number two: super casual appearance even though she can afford to dress like a model. Kristy likes to wear jeans, a T-shirt or turtleneck, and sneakers. Her shoulder-length brown hair is usually back in a ponytail. Sometimes she wears a baseball cap. I've never seen her wear makeup. Her carelessness about her appearance seems like an opposite because her stepfather, Watson, is a millionaire!

Kristy's father abandoned the family not long after her younger brother, David Michael, was born. She has two older brothers, Sam and Charlie, which meant there were four kids for Mrs. Thomas to support on her own. It wasn't easy, but she managed. Then, not long ago, she met Watson, fell in love, and married him.

After the wedding, Kristy's family moved into Watson's mansion, which is in a different part of Stoneybrook from the Thomases' old house. (They used to live across the street from Claudia, here on Bradford Court.) And just as Kristy's house became much bigger, her family did, too. Watson has two kids from his first marriage, Karen and Andrew, who are seven and four. They live with Watson every other month. Both of them adore Kristy and she adores them back.

Kristy's also crazy about Emily Michelle, her newest sibling. Emily's from Vietnam. Watson and Kristy's mother adopted her shortly after they were married. She's two and a half now. Nannie, Kristy's grandmother, moved in soon after Emily came home. She helps to look after Emily during working hours.

I'll tell you about Shannon next, since she's Kristy's across-the-street neighbor. When they first met, Kristy thought Shannon was a snob.

But Kristy soon discovered that Shannon isn't snobby at all.

Shannon's family (which consists of her mom, her dad, and her two younger sisters) breeds their pedigreed Bernese mountain dog. When Kristy's dog, Louie, died, Shannon gave Kristy a Bernese pup. Kristy named the puppy Shannon. From then on, they were friends.

Shannon has great hair. It's curly, blonde, and thick. She has blue eyes, high cheekbones, and a ski-jump nose.

Since Shannon goes to a different school than I do, I'm still getting to know her, so I can't tell you *that* much about her. I know she's a good student and very involved in school activities. So far, she's done a great job of filling in for Dawn.

Speaking of Dawn, I'll tell you about her, even though at the moment she's in California. Dawn moved here with her mother and her younger brother, Jeff, after her parents divorced. Mrs. Schafer was originally from Stoneybrook. They moved into an old farmhouse (built in 1795) on Burnt Hill Road. Jeff was never really happy here. He went back to live with his father in California pretty quickly. Dawn had trouble adjusting to the cold weather, but, mostly, she liked Stoneybrook.

I think Dawn is totally gorgeous. She's tall and thin with long, white-blonde hair. Dawn is seriously into ecology and healthy food. She eats no red meat, no junk food. She actually *enjoys* stuff like tofu and seaweed salad. No matter how much the rest of us kid her or pretend to gag, she just keeps on eating it.

Like Kristy, Dawn is now part of a blended family. The great part is that her family joined up with the family of her very best friend, Mary Anne Spier, who's also a BSC member.

Things get the tiniest bit complicated here, so let me take a moment to tell you about Mary Anne before I go on with the rest of Dawn's story.

Mary Anne and Kristy used to live next door to one another on Bradford Court. Mary Anne lived alone with her father; her mother had died when Mary Anne was very young. Her father had very rigid ideas about bringing up a daughter. Mary Anne had to obey strict rules about everything from how long she could talk on the phone to what she could wear. (She still wore braids and jumpers in the seventh grade!)

Then Mary Anne met Dawn, who had only been in Stoneybrook for four days. They didn't appear to have much in common. Dawn is tall, Mary Anne is short. Dawn is a cool dresser, Mary Anne wasn't. Dawn is outgoing, Mary

18

Anne is shy. But, still, they became good friends pretty quickly.

One day, as they browsed through Mrs. Schafer's old high school yearbook, they discovered something amazing. Mrs. Schafer and Mr. Spier had been boyfriend and girlfriend in high school! Obviously, they hadn't gotten married, at least not to each other. But now they were both free again. Mary Anne and Dawn decided to try to get their parents back together.

It took some doing, but finally everything fell into place. After dating for a long time, Mr. Spier and Mrs. Schafer got married. That's how Dawn and Mary Anne became stepsisters, and Mary Anne and her dad moved into the farmhouse on Burnt Hill Road. At first, it wasn't easy. Everyone — including Mary Anne and Dawn — had a bumpy time learning to work together as a family. But, things slowly started settling down. And, just when everything was finally going smoothly, Dawn decided she missed Jeff and her dad, and went to California to stay with them. Dawn swears she'll be back, but I sometimes wonder. We all really miss her, and hope she doesn't decide to stay in California.

Oh! Talking about Mary Anne reminded me of someone else you should know about: Logan Bruno, Mary Anne's steady boyfriend.

The reason you should know about him is that he's an associate BSC member, like Shannon used to be. We call Logan whenever we have more jobs than we can handle. Logan has curly light brown hair and a Southern accent. His family (which includes his mother and father, a younger sister, and a younger brother) is from Louisville, Kentucky.

Let's see, who haven't I mentioned? Claudia! Claudia Kishi, whose room we were in at that moment, is strikingly beautiful. She has long, silky black hair, and lovely almond-shaped eyes. (She's Japanese-American.) Claudia's natural beauty is set off by her unique fashion sense. You see, Claudia is extremely artistic. She paints, sculpts, makes jewelry and pottery, sketches — you name it. And her clothing reflects her artistic nature. She combines colors and styles in an original way which really works. For example, today she wore wide-legged maroon corduroy pants, a yellow paisley-print blouse with ruffle sleeves, and a yellow-and-maroon-striped vest. Her hair was fixed in two braids and she wore a black brimmed fisherman's cap. On her feet were heavy-soled black Doc Marten shoes with bright yellow laces. It might sound a little strange, but on her it looked spectacular.

Looking at Claudia's creamy skin and slim

figure, you'd never guess she's a junk food fanatic. Bags of snacks are stashed all over her room, because her parents disapprove of this habit. They also disapprove of the Nancy Drew books Claudia adores. (Those are hidden all over the place, too.) Claudia's parents would like her to read more "challenging" books, and be more like her older sister, Janine. Janine is an authentic genius, with an I.Q. of 196. Claudia is smart, too, but there's no way she'll ever be like Janine. For one thing, Claudia isn't much of a student. She does just enough work to get by and no more.

Claudia's best friend is Stacey McGill, another BSC member. Stacey is our New York girl. She's a real live native New Yorker, and she loves everything about New York City. Like Claudia, Stacey also has a great fashion sense, although she isn't quite as original. Her blonde hair is permed and she has the biggest blue eyes.

As I mentioned, Jessi and I joined the BSC when Stacey moved back to New York. While they were there Stacey's parents decided to divorce. Soon afterward, Stacey moved to Stoneybrook once again with her mother, and rejoined the BSC.

Considering all the moves she's made and her parents' divorce, Stacey is a remarkably upbeat person. That's even more surprising when you consider that she has another problem. Stacey has a very serious form of diabetes. Diabetes is a condition which prevents your body from properly regulating the sugar levels in your bloodstream. To keep her diabetes under control, Stacey has to monitor her diet carefully (no sweets). She must also give herself insulin injections every day.

Now that you know who is who, let me give you a brief rundown on how the BSC works. We meet in Claudia's room, because she is the only one of us with her own phone and a private number. Her private number allows us to do business without tying up someone's family phone. Because we use her phone and room, Claudia is the vice-president.

At the beginning of every meeting, Kristy, who is president, asks if there is any new business. If anyone has something special to discuss that's when we do it.

Kristy is president because the club was her idea, and also because she is the driving force that keeps things going smoothly. She runs the club strictly, like a real business. And she's constantly coming up with great new ideas. Kid-Kits, for example. Kid-Kits are boxes filled with our old toys and books, plus new art supplies and stuff. We don't bring them on every baby-sitting job, but kids love them when we do. The BSC notebook is another of

Kristy's ideas. It's a book in which we record what happens on all of our sitting jobs. It's a great reference if you are sitting for a family for the first time, or if you want to know what's been happening with certain kids since the last time you sat for them. Some members grumble about having to write in it, but I love to. (Naturally, since I love to write.)

When Claudia's phone rings, the person sitting nearest answers, and takes down the client's information. She tells the client we'll call right back, and then asks Mary Anne who can take the job.

Mary Anne is the club secretary. She keeps the record book in order. The record book lists everyone's schedules (my orthodontist appointments, Jessi's ballet classes, Stacey's doctor appointments, etc.). It also contains information about our clients — addresses, rates paid, plus records of our charges' allergies or any special problems.

By checking the record book, Mary Anne can figure out which of us is free to take a particular job. Once we decide who will take it, we call the client back.

Stacey is the club treasurer. She's a math whiz, which makes her the natural choice for the job. She collects the dues and keeps the money in a big manila envelope. We use the money to help pay Claudia's phone bill, and to pay Kristy's brother, Charlie, to drive Kristy and Shannon to meetings, since they live so far away. We also use the money to restock our Kid-Kits from time to time. If there's any money left over (sometimes there is, thanks to Stacey's good money management) we put it toward something fun such as a pizza party or a slumber party.

These days, Shannon is the alternate officer (that's usually Dawn's job). The alternate officer must know everyone's job, so that she can fill in if anyone is absent. Jessi and I are called junior officers, but we don't have any special duties.

At this particular meeting, the phone didn't start ringing until about a quarter to six. No one had any new business either. So, while Claudia passed around a bag of Doritos, and Mary Anne wrote in the club notebook, I told the others about Jessi's and my English assignment. "Does anyone have any good ideas for us?" I asked.

"I have an idea for Jessi," said Stacey. "Why don't you write down the stories of some famous ballets? Sometimes when I go to the ballet with my father at Lincoln Center, I have no idea what the story is. I mean, the dancing is gorgeous and all, but it would be nice to understand the story behind the dance. You could make a book of the stories."

"What a great idea!" said Jessi. "I could do *Swan Lake*, *The Nutcracker*, and *The Firebird*!"

"And you wouldn't have to interview Madame Noelle," I said, laughing.

"She can be a little intimidating," Jessi agreed. "But I like the idea of telling the stories. I can write about how they make me feel and how the feelings behind the stories affect my dancing."

"Mal, why don't you just write another story?" Mary Anne suggested.

"I was thinking I'd like to do something with kids," I told her. "After all, I do want to write for kids. I was thinking of working with the Kids Can Do Anything Club at the elementary school, but I'm not sure what to do."

"Kids, huh," Kristy mused. "Why don't you write a play? A play featuring kids. Maybe you could get the Kids Club to perform your play."

"I like that," I agreed excitedly. "I like it a lot." Good old Kristy. You can always count on her for a great idea.

CHAPTER 3

On Monday, after school, I headed over to Stoneybrook Elementary. I wanted to talk to Mr. Katz and Ms. Simon, who run the Kids Club. I was eager to find out what they thought about my writing a play for the kids to perform.

When I reached the classroom where the club meets, room 164, I peeked through the window in the door. Becca, Haley, and several other kids, some of whom I know from around the neighborhood and from baby-sitting, were busily sorting through boxes of canned goods. Mr. Katz was sitting in a chair, making checks on a paper attached to his clipboard. It looked as if their Thanksgiving food drive was well underway.

"Mallory," said a woman, coming up behind me in the hall. It was Ms. Simon. "How nice to see you. What brings you here?"

"Hi, Ms. Simon," I replied. "Actually, I

came to see you. You and Mr. Katz."

"Great. Just to say hello?"

"No, I mean, not only to say hello. I have to do a project for English and I thought I'd write a play and have the kids in the Kids Club perform it."

I hadn't intended to just blurt out my idea while standing in the hallway like that. But that's how it came out. I studied Ms. Simon's expression, looking for a reaction.

Ms. Simon nodded thoughtfully. "What will the play be about?"

"Um, I haven't actually gotten that far yet," I admitted. "Does it matter?"

"Well, for one thing, I'd like the kids to learn something from it."

"But isn't being in a play a learning experience?" I asked. It hadn't occurred to me that the teachers might turn me down. "They learn how to act, and speak in front of a group, and make costumes, and a lot of helpful things like that."

"You're right," Ms. Simon agreed hesitantly. "More important, though, Mallory, the Kids Can Do Anything Club is a service oriented group. I'm not sure how putting on a play fits in with that."

"Well . . ." I pressed my lips together as I tried to think of something persuasive to say. Luckily, a stroke of genius came my way right then. "People in hospitals and nursing homes love to see plays. If the kids learned how to put on their own plays, they'd be able to entertain people in those places. That's a very valuable service."

Ms. Simon's eyes brightened with enthusiasm. "That is brilliant, Mallory!" (I agreed.) "The food drive is wrapping up. Mr. Katz and I were wondering what to do next. With the holidays coming soon, we can put together a show, and travel to spots where people can't get out."

"That would be great," I said. "But, well, I wanted to write the play."

"Yes, of course. They can do your play to learn about plays. And then they can put their own together. It think this might just work out beautifully. Would you be willing to work with interested kids on the topic of drama, of telling a story through dialogue, and so forth? If we can shape this as a real learning experience it would be wonderful."

How could I say no? Besides, it sounded like fun. "Sure, that sounds good," I agreed.

"Let me discuss this with Mr. Katz. If he agrees, and I think he will, we'll arrange for you to come in and talk to the kids at the next meeting. How does that sound?"

"Cool," I replied happily. "I'll start working on a talk."

"Wonderful! I'll call you up tomorrow afternoon and we can discuss it some more," said Ms. Simon.

"Thanks!" I said, smiling.

That night I lay on my bed and worked on my proposal for Mr. Williams. *Although I plan to write books for kids, I might like to try playwriting for them, as well. Writing a play for kids will be a new experience for me,* I wrote. *A writer must always grow and expand as an artist. I am looking forward to this project because it will open me to a new experience in writing.* I thought that sounded pretty good. I wrote another page which wasn't entirely honest. I said that watching the kids work on the play would give me a good chance to observe kids and see how they acted and felt, which would help in my writing. True, it *would* give me that experience, but I didn't exactly have to put on a play in order to observe kids. Between my brothers and sisters and the kids I sit for I have tons of kids to watch. Still, I wanted to make this project seem highly educational.

The next day I handed in my proposal, ahead of time. That afternoon, Ms. Simon called to tell me that Mr. Katz was wild about the idea of my working on drama with the kids. They wanted me to come in the following Wednesday.

I felt confident that Mr. Williams would be

equally wild about my proposal. "Mallory, could you see me after class, please?" he requested the following morning.

"Sure," I replied.

I spent the rest of class thinking of cool ways to react to his praise without blushing or smiling too much. I imagined Mr. Williams saying something like: "Mallory, this is the most original idea any sixth-grader has ever submitted to me. I am awestruck!"

I could then nod knowingly and reply: "I appreciate your support. My first book will be dedicated to you because so few teachers encourage the talent of an original thinker."

No, that might be a bit much. Maybe a simple "thank you" would be best.

When class ended I approached Mr. Williams's desk. "Mallory, I want to speak to you about your proposal," he said.

Without meaning to, I began smiling. It's hard not to smile when you know praise is headed your way.

"It just isn't right," he said.

"What?"

"It's a good beginning, but it has to be developed further. As it stands now, it's not involved enough. It's not really sufficiently career-related, either."

"But it's writing for kids, and I want to be a kids' writer," I objected.

"Yes, I understand that. But, I'm looking for something which will enhance your understanding of the career you've chosen. I don't think you'll learn anything new from this."

When he put it that way, I couldn't think of anything new I'd learn, either. (Obviously he hadn't fallen for the part about my having a chance to observe kids.) Maybe that was what I'd liked about the project to begin with — I already knew how to do it. Even though I'd never written a play, I'd read a lot of them. I was sure I could write one. It seemed pretty easy.

"Take this back," said Mr. Williams, handing me my proposal. "Try to think of ways to make it more challenging to yourself. Come up with something you'd like to learn and then set out to learn it."

"All right," I agreed glumly.

"I know you'll come up with something good. I have a lot of faith in you, Mallory."

"Thank you," I said. (I had certainly been right about that being the best reply.)

It was a good thing Mr. Williams had faith in me, because by Thursday afternoon I'd lost faith in myself — or at least, faith in my ability to come up with an interesting project. I hated the thought of giving up on my play. I wanted to do it, and besides, I'd already promised to work with the Kids Club on a drama project. I couldn't back out of that now. There had to be a way to make my proposal bigger and more exciting. But what was it?

The proposal was due the next morning, so I had to come up with something by that night. I sat with my back against my bed and stared down at the blank lined paper in the notebook propped against my knees. The pad accurately reflected what was in my head — nothing. (The pad was really better off. At least *it* had blue lines. My mind was a *total* blank!) What could I do to make this project more impressive?

Absently, I began doodling on the pad. (Doodling sometimes helps me think.) I drew a picture of Alice Anderson, at least the way I imagined her in *Alice Anderson*. There were no pictures in Henrietta Hayes's book, but the cover showed her as a pretty girl with long, wavy, corn-colored hair, running happily through a meadow of wild flowers. It was a nice picture, but I wished that inside the book the reader could see more of Alice in different situations.

"What are you doing?" asked Vanessa coming into our room.

"Trying to think of something to do for my English project," I grumbled.

Vanessa gazed down at my pad. "Who is that supposed to be?"

"Alice Anderson. A character from a book I just finished."

Vanessa dropped a long white envelope down on the pad. "Here. Mom sent me up to give you this. She said you'd want to see it right away. Who is it from?"

Turning the letter over in my hand, I saw it had no return address on it, but it did have a name written in the upper lefthand corner. Henrietta Hayes!

Henrietta Hayes had written back to me in just one week! Awesome! Unbelievable! I tore open the envelope.

The letter was neatly typed. It said: *Dear Reader, Thanks so much for your lovely letter. I am very glad that you enjoyed my book. Hearing from you means a lot. I'll try to answer some of the questions as best I can.* In the next couple of paragraphs I learned several facts about Ms. Hayes. For example, she was born in Binghamton, New York, and she graduated from Ithaca College.

What I found most interesting was that Henrietta Hayes was both an author and a playwright. She'd written five Alice Anderson books, six other books, and ten plays.

By the time I was done with the letter (which

Vanessa insisted I read aloud), I knew a lot more about Henrietta Hayes. I realized, though, that the letter didn't answer any of the questions I'd asked.

This puzzled me for a moment, until I realized something. Henrietta Hayes probably sent the same letter to everyone who wrote to her. That's why it said Dear Reader, not Dear Mallory.

"She didn't write this to me," I said glumly.

"Then whose letter is it?" Vanessa asked.

"The letter is mine," I replied. "But it wasn't written to me, specifically."

"It says Mallory Pike on the envelope," Vanessa pointed out.

"I mean she writes the same thing to everyone!" I cried, losing patience with Vanessa.

"Oh," said Vanessa. "I get it. I guess she has to answer a lot of letters. It was nice of her to write back, though."

What Vanessa said was true. It *was* nice of her to answer, and so quickly, too. I wondered how the letter reached me so fast. Maybe Henrietta Hayes lived close by. I checked the postmark on the envelope, to see where it had been mailed from.

Close by were not the words! The letter was postmarked from Stamford, Connecticut!

Henrietta Hayes lived in Stamford, the closest city to Stoneybrook! At any rate, she had mailed the letter from Stamford.

This new information gave me a brilliant idea. I might be able to contact Henrietta Hayes, maybe even talk to her on the phone! I could ask what it was like to be an author. Where did her ideas come from? Was it difficult to write? How did she get her first book published? How did she feel when she saw her first play performed?

Meanwhile, I'd write and direct my own play. I would experience being a playwright, just like Henrietta Hayes. Then I'd write a paper about my experiences, and how they compared to Henrietta Hayes's experiences.

It was so simple, yet so brilliant I almost couldn't believe I'd thought of it!

"Vanessa, I need to be alone now," I said. "I just had a great idea for my proposal and I have to write it down."

"Okay," Vanessa agreed, and she headed for the door. "What are you going to do it on?"

"The life of my new favorite author, Henrietta Hayes, and how it compares and contrasts with the life of up-and-coming soon-to-be-famous author and playwright, Mallory Pike."

I began writing feverishly, full of enthusiasm. This time I not only had a proposal I knew Mr. Williams would love, but one that I felt incredibly excited and confident about, as well.

CHAPTER 4

What a blast to be back at the elumantiry skhool! It made me feel so old — anchint! Seeing the kids at the KCDAC was fun, two. Mal was grate with them. I'm glad she talked me into coming with her. I even lerned a fuw things aboot drama, myself!

One week later on the following Wednesday, Claudia came with me to the Kids Club meeting. I hadn't really talked her into it. She'd volunteered during our last BSC meeting when I'd told everybody about my project, and admitted to being a little nervous about talking to the club members by myself.

When we stepped into the classroom, it was zoo city. The kids were laughing, throwing wadded paper balls, and poking one another. The noise was pretty intense. "Oh my gosh, they're wild!" Claudia gasped, looking at me with a worried expression.

"Jessi warned me about this," I told her. "She said it's no problem." Once, when Ms. Simon had to be away for a few weeks, Jessi had filled in for her, helping Mr. Katz with the club. Mr. Katz had told her that the kids need to blow off some steam after being cooped up at their desks all day. He lets them run wild for about five minutes before starting the meetings.

"Hi, girls," Mr. Katz greeted us.

"Hi," I replied. "This is my friend, Claudia Kishi. She's going to help me work with the kids, if that's okay."

"Terrific," said Mr. Katz.

Ms. Simon approached from the back of the classroom. She already knew Claudia because she'd once had her as a student. "Hi, Mallory. Nice to see you again, Claudia. The kids are very excited about this," she told us. "And so are Mr. Katz and I. Would you like to get started?"

"Sure," I replied, suddenly feeling scared.

Claudia squeezed my arm gently and smiled. "You'll be great."

I smiled back at her, not so sure.

Mr. Katz clapped his hands and the kids instantly came to order, seating themselves toward the front of the room. Ms. Simon introduced Claudia and me. "Mallory is here to talk to you about acting and playwriting," Mr. Katz told the kids. "You'll have the chance to try out for a play she is writing. And then Mallory will help us put together a holiday play to perform in hospitals and nursing homes."

The club members applauded, which was very sweet.

From my school pack, I took out index cards I'd prepared the night before. I'd written notes about what I wanted to say. On one card I'd tried to lay out the difference between a play and other forms of writing, namely that a play has to be told through dialogue with very little narration.

I talked about how acting something out was different from just reading lines, about how you had to be expressive and try to pretend you were the character. I had also made an index card with notes on what kinds of plays people who were shut in might like to see. (In my opinion they should be happy plays, not sad ones.)

Claudia later told me that while she listened to my talk, she was gazing around the room at the kids. She said they were super interested.

Of course, she knew some of the kids because she'd baby-sat for them. Naturally, she knew Charlotte Johanssen very well, since the Johanssens are regular BSC clients. Char sat crammed into one seat with Becca. And Haley scooted her desk in beside them. The three of them are pretty close friends.

Near Haley, Claudia spotted a girl she didn't know well, but whom she'd heard of from Jessi. It was Danielle Roberts, who was listening to me talk, bright-eyed with interest. When Jessi had been working with the club, she told us how Danielle had been diagnosed with leukemia the summer after third grade. She returned to the club in fourth grade, after spending a lot of time in the hospital and undergoing chemotherapy.

Chemotherapy is a way of fighting cancer (leukemia is cancer of the blood) with powerful drugs. The drugs are so powerful that they can make some people nauseated, and even make their hair fall out. Both of those things had happened to Danielle.

When Danielle returned to school she was thin from being sick and wore a scarf to hide her bald head. She had dark circles under her eyes, and looked generally run-down.

Claudia was able to identify Danielle because not long ago, Jessi told us Danielle's leukemia had come back and she was again undergoing chemotherapy. Claudia could tell, just by looking, that she wasn't well. Still, Claudia admired the way Danielle didn't spend time feeling sorry for herself. Despite her own serious problem, she was there at the KCDAC meeting, thinking about how she could help others.

Once I started my speech, I found that it was easier than I'd expected. I got so excited about the subject that I forgot my nervousness. The words just flowed out of me. "I'd love for you to help me with my play," I concluded. "And thanks for listening."

The club members applauded again, which made me feel good. "Now you kids have a decision to make," Ms. Simon told them. "You can either work with Mallory and Claudia on a play, or with Mr. Katz and me on making holiday decorations. We've decided that when we take our play to hospitals and nursing homes, we'll also take a holiday party, and leave behind some decorations to brighten the places."

"What a great idea!" Claudia spoke up impulsively. Later that afternoon, Claudia told me that the notion of working on holiday crafts projects had appealed to her immediately. But, at the time, I didn't realize I was in danger of losing my assistant to the crafts half of the room.

"Who wants to work on decorations?" Ms. Simon asked. About half of the club members did. "Then the rest of these guys are yours, Mallory," said Ms. Simon. "Why don't you meet with them in the back of the class."

Claudia and I moved to the back. "Pull your chairs into a circle," Claudia instructed them. As they did, I surveyed my cast. I had Haley, Becca, Char, and Danielle. Sara Hill, another of our baby-sitting charges was there. So was Buddy Barrett, whom we sit for pretty often. Three boys and a girl I didn't know at all had also joined the group. That made ten kids, which seemed like a good, manageable number for a first-time playwright (and now director) like myself.

"I haven't written my play yet," I told them. "But I want to get a sense of how you read." I took a small stack of yellow paperback playscripts from my pack. The middle school library keeps a number of copies of certain plays, in case a class or club wants to put on a production.

The scripts were for a play called *Ain't Life Grand*, written by — Henrietta Hayes! It was the second play she'd published. I'd read it through in one night. Like *Alice Anderson*, it was very funny, and left you with a warm, happy feeling when it was done.

Claudia passed the books out and I assigned each kid a role. Slowly, we went through the script, with each kid reading his or her part.

Sara Hill was good, and so were Becca and Char, especially considering how shy they are. Buddy Barret was good, too. Claudia reminded me that he'd been great when the BSC was involved in a school production of "Peter Pan."

Haley and the rest of the kids were somewhere in the middle. But Danielle really shone. She read well, with lots of expression.

The time flew by. Before we were done with the first act, the meeting was over. "I may not have my play written by next week," I told the kids. "If I don't, we'll do some acting exercises." Along with the plays, I'd found a book on acting in the library. It was full of fun ways to practice acting, such as improvising skits, pretending to be someone's image in a mirror, and stuff like that.

Claudia collected the scripts and said good-bye to the kids. Ms. Simon and Mr. Katz thanked us as we left the room. "What did you think?" I asked Claudia when we were in the hall.

"Your speech was great. And the kids should be good. What will your play be about, though?"

"Good question," I replied. "I think writers usually write about things they know, about their lives."

"You mean, you think most writing is autobiographical?" asked Claudia.

"I do," I said, warming to my subject. "I really do. Take Henrietta Hayes for example. I have now read almost half of her books. I'm nearly positive that she must be either Alice Anderson or Alice Anderson's mother. Her characters are so real they have to be from her life."

"At the meeting last Monday, when you were telling about how you changed your project, you said you'd written to Henrietta Hayes. Has she written back to you yet?" Claudia asked.

"Yes, but she hasn't answered my second letter." After my brainstorm, I'd written to her in care of her publishing company again. This time I'd explained that I lived close to her and needed her help with a school project. I said I'd be willing to go to her house and

44

interview her if that was possible. Considering how quickly she'd returned my letter the last time, I expected to hear from her soon.

"From the way you described it, it sounds like a great project," said Claudia as we walked out of school.

"Well, Mr. Williams liked it this time. This morning he gave me the go-ahead to work on it. He said this proposal was a big improvement over the first one, and he really seemed to like the part about Henrietta Hayes."

"But what will you do if she doesn't contact you?" Claudia asked.

"Oh, she will. I'm pretty sure," I said confidently. I had a very strong feeling that my letter would capture her interest this time. From her books, Henrietta Hayes didn't seem like the kind of woman who would leave a kid stuck when it came to a school project.

Claudia walked home with me. I invited her in for some hot cocoa and brownies Mom had made. (Of course, Ms. Sweettooth Claudia agreed to that!) We would have just enough time to eat before heading over to her house for our BSC meeting.

When I opened my front door, things looked pretty calm, at least for our house. Margo and Claire were playing Chutes and Ladders on the living room floor. Vanessa was brushing

Pow, who sat contentedly on the rug beside her.

"You're not supposed to do that in the living room," I reminded Vanessa as Claudia and I went past.

"He's hardly shedding," Vanessa replied. (I had a strong feeling that her idea of "hardly shedding" and Mom's wouldn't be the same.) "Mal, there's another letter for you from that Harriet lady who didn't really write to you the last time," Vanessa added. "Mom put it on the kitchen table."

"Henrietta Hayes!" I cried, dashing into the kitchen. The letter was on the table. In a flash, I tore it open.

"What does it say?" Claudia asked excitedly.

"Dear Reader," I began glumly. "Thanks so much for your lovely letter."

It was the exact same form letter I'd received the last time. Now what was I supposed to do?

CHAPTER 5

That night I lay under my covers with a flashlight beaming down on the pages of *Alice Anderson's Big Break*, the fourth Alice Anderson book. In this book, Alice's oldest brother, Lars, drives her all the way to Hollywood in his hot-rod car because Alice has been offered a job as the nanny to the kids of a famous Hollywood director.

Once she's there, Alice does everything possible to show the director she's really a talented actress. (For instance, she tries to work Shakespearian quotations into her conversations with him. He'd ask, "Who just called, Alice?" and she'd answer, from *Romeo and Juliet*, "What's in a name? That which we call a rose by any other name would smell as sweet.") The director is not impressed. In fact, he gets annoyed and finally fires Alice. On her way out the door, she makes one last effort: "Parting is such sweet sorrow."

I didn't want to wake Vanessa, but it was hard not to laugh out loud. I kept reading, biting down on my laughter, until I came to a scene so funny I just couldn't hold it back any more. Lars boosts Alice through a window onto a movie set. She falls into a barrel of paste in the costume room. Then, she stumbles onto a pile of feather boas. At that point, Alice smells smoke, and realizes the costume room is on fire. With feathers stuck all over her, she races onto the movie set, and right into the arms of this superstar named Harrison Lloyd. He says, "Nobody told me there was an ostrich in this scene." The way Henrietta Hayes told the story made it so funny that I couldn't help laughing out loud. Luckily, Vanessa didn't wake up.

I read until midnight, all the way to the last scene, where Alice and Lars sit up laughing about the adventure as Alice plucks feathers from herself. She hugs Lars and thanks him for being the best big brother in the world. Lars replies, "You're worth the trouble, Alice."

Somehow I just couldn't picture the triplets and Nicky gazing fondly at me and saying, "You're worth the trouble, Mallory!" That picture simply wouldn't form in my head.

I wished the Pike family were more like the Anderson family. My family is always interrupting, making noise, and disturbing me when I'm trying to write. My brothers and sisters only worry about their own problems, not mine. The Andersons were so warm and caring. They never insulted or teased one another. They always helped each other. My family is all right, I suppose. I mean, I love them and all. But we sure aren't the Andersons.

As I shut the book my mind raced. If Alice Anderson had to find an author, and couldn't, what would she do? When Alice couldn't get through a door, she went in a window. She never let anything stop her. Alice Anderson would find Henrietta Hayes somehow.

And so would I!

I thought hard. The publishing company was located in New York City, but the postmark on both of Ms. Hayes's letters was Stamford. What did that tell me? It told me the form letter didn't come from the publishing company. It must have come from Henrietta Hayes, herself. The company must send the letters on to her.

Tossing off my blanket, I tiptoed out of my dark room. The flashlight beam guided me down to the living room, where I opened a cabinet door and pulled out the fat yellow area phone book. If Ms. Hayes lived around Stamford, her name and address might be in this book. The book covered the towns near Stamford.

The first thing I learned is that Hayes is an extremely popular last name. There was almost an entire page of them.

But there was only one Henrietta! And she was right there in the phone book.

I stared at her name happily. How unbelievably great!

My eyes traveled over to her address, and I nearly fell to the floor. Henrietta Hayes lived on Morgan Road, in Stoneybrook! Morgan Road is off Burnt Hill Road. Dawn's and Mary Anne's house is on Burnt Hill Road. Logan lives on Burnt Hill, too.

All this time Logan, Dawn, and Mary Anne had been Henrietta Hayes's neighbors and they didn't even know it!

The important thing was that I'd found her. With the phone book in my arms, I went back upstairs to my room. By flashlight, I wrote Henrietta Hayes a third letter.

Dear Ms. Hayes, I've just finished reading Alice Anderson's Big Break. It is the funniest book I've ever read. I'm sad that there is only one more Alice book left for me to read.

I really hope you are working on more. Since
I've discovered your work, I've become your
number one fan. You may already know all
this because I've written you before. My
problem is that this time, I need you to write
me back a real letter. It's important because
my class project, which counts for almost my
whole grade for this marking period, depends
on it.

I went on to tell her about the project. I told
her every detail, about how Mr. Williams
hadn't liked it until I added the part about
comparing and contrasting my experience as
an author with her own. (I wanted her to know
she was a big part of this.) I mentioned that
we were neighbors and that I had friends who
lived close to her on Burnt Hill Road. (I
thought that might appeal to her sense of
neighborliness.) By the time the letter was finished, it was three pages long. For a finishing
touch, I wrote out an envelope with my name
and address on it. *P.S.* I added to the bottom
of my letter. *This self-addressed stamped envelope
is enclosed for your convenience. I hope you can write
back soon since time is running out.*

I stuck the letter in an envelope and added
my return reply envelope. In the morning, I'd
find two stamps.

When I was done, I felt suddenly exhausted. I crawled into bed and had an odd dream. I dreamed I was Alice Anderson, walking up Morgan Road looking for Henrietta Hayes. I found her house, which in my dream was a huge castle with a moat. As I crossed the drawbridge, it started to go up. I tried to jump off, but my sweater got stuck to the end of the drawbridge. As I dangled helplessly from the end of the drawbridge I called, "Help! Henrietta Hayes? Help me!"

I don't remember what happened after that, but in the morning I awoke full of energy. "What are you so hyper about this morning?" asked Vanessa, as I dashed around the room getting dressed.

"I have lots to do," I replied. "I have to mail a letter and start working on my play today. It's just a busy day, that's all."

"Wow, you're turbo-charged," said Vanessa, rolling over in bed.

I did feel turbo-charged (whatever that means, exactly). I got two stamps from my mother and wrote *super important* on the outside of the envelope in red. On the way to school with Jessi, I mailed my letter to Henrietta Hayes's home address.

"I don't think she could miss that letter," Jessi laughed as she saw me put the letter in the box.

"I hope not," I said. "Can you believe she lives right here in Stoneybrook?"

"That's pretty cool," Jessi agreed.

During English, I asked for a pass to go to the library. I returned *Alice Anderson's Big Break*, and took out *Alice Anderson's Greatest Challenge*. I also found two more plays by Henrietta Hayes, "The Happiest Day," and "Frog Pond Vacation." In the same section I found a book entitled, *The Basics of Playwriting*. I grabbed it from the shelf and took it over to a table along with my other books.

I opened *The Basics of Playwriting*, interested in what the author had to say. *The writer Ernest Hemingway was not a playwright,* read the opening lines of the introduction. *But his idea that authors should write about what they know is valuable for playwrights as well as novelists. Sticking to familiar material enables a writer to imbue his or her work with a realistic quality which might otherwise be missing. Many successful modern writers have taken Hemingway's advice. The beginning writer, too, would do well to heed this suggestion.*

There it was! I'd been right. It was just as I'd said to Claudia the other day. Most people write about themselves. It made me so eager to know more about Henrietta Hayes. What a happy, funny person she must be!

Would she ever write back to me?

I sighed so loudly that the librarian shot me a warning glance.

Well, there was no sense worrying about it. Instead, I had to make the best use of my time while I waited. The best thing I could do was start writing my own play. What would I write about, though?

I looked again at the book open in front of me, quickly rereading the opening paragraph. That's when it hit me. Like Henrietta Hayes's address, the perfect subject was right in my own home. The Pike family!

CHAPTER 6

A sick feeling churned in my stomach four days later as I stood in my front hall and read the words in front of me. *Dear Reader, Thanks so much for your lovely letter. . . .*

What did it take to get through to this woman?

No wonder she replied so fast. She didn't even read her letters! If she'd read my letter she'd have known I was getting desperate!

I'd nearly finished reading *Alice Anderson's Greatest Challenge.* As in the previous books, Alice never let anything defeat her. Last night I had read a chapter in which Alice storms into a producer's office and demands to be allowed to audition for the role in a big movie. The producer is so impressed with her spunk that he agrees.

With Alice in mind, I ran upstairs and grabbed a notebook. I also snapped up the questionnaire I'd prepared in order to be ready the very moment Ms. Hayes contacted me. I put them in my pack and hurried back downstairs.

"Where are you going?" Mom called to me from the kitchen as I pulled on my jacket and headed for the front door.

"To Morgan Road," I replied firmly.

"What's on Morgan Road?" Mom wanted to know.

"I'm going to find Henrietta Hayes," I called over my shoulder as I swung out the door.

In the garage, I grabbed my bike and pedaled to the street. A few minutes later, I turned onto Burnt Hill Road. I spotted Mary Anne in her yard, raking leaves.

"Hi," she called to me. I really didn't want to be delayed. (I worried I'd lose my nerve.) I just waved and kept going. When she realized I wasn't stopping she called out, "Where are you going?"

"To meet Henrietta Hayes," I called back.

"Good luck!" she shouted. At the last BSC meeting I'd told my friends about Henrietta Hayes living on Morgan Road. Mary Anne had told me then that 312 had to be all the way at the end of Morgan Road since the house nearest Burnt Hill Road was only number 80.

Burnt Hill Road is some hill! I breathed hard as I pumped past the old barn behind Mary Anne and Dawn's house. (There's a secret passage which leads from Dawn's bedroom out to the barn. Isn't that cool?) By the time I reached the top of the hill, I was panting like crazy. (I told you I'm not exactly a super athlete.) I still had a way to go. Luckily, the rest of the road curved downhill.

Well, not exactly all downhill. There were small ups and downs along the way.

Morgan Road was the fifth left turn off Burnt Hill Road. It was winding and hilly, too. Eventually, though, I reached 310 Morgan Road. It was a big, fancy house. So was 314, the next house I came to. What had happened to 312?

Then I spotted a narrow dirt path which led into a cluster of trees. I peered in, trying to see what lay behind the trees. The trees were too close together, though. On a hunch, I turned my bike down the path.

Soon, I entered the line of trees. There, in the woods, stood 312 Morgan Road. Henrietta Hayes certainly didn't live in a castle. But I liked her house. It was a cozy-looking one-story, mostly brown wood except for a stone chimney up the side. A screened-in porch on the right led to a wooden deck with several bird feeders on it.

I got off my bike and I walked it up the stone path leading to the house. For a second, I almost lost my nerve, feeling more like chicken Mallory Pike than indomitable Alice

Anderson. Breathing a gulp of air for courage, I pressed on to the front door.

I didn't see a doorbell anywhere, so I pulled open the screen door and knocked hard on the heavy wooden inside door. Then I quickly shut the screen door and stepped back. I didn't want Henrietta Hayes to think I was walking right into her house or anything like that.

I waited . . . and waited. Finally, I decided that Henrietta Hayes wasn't home. I took my questionnaire from my pack. I'd leave it inside her screen door, along with a note.

I leaned up against her house and began writing my note. At that moment, the door opened. Dropping my pad, I jumped back, startled.

"Can I help you?" asked the short, petite woman in the doorway. She wore brown-framed glasses with thick lenses, which made it hard to see her eyes. Her pale face would have looked young except for the fine wrinkles lining it. She had thick gray and brown hair which was cut to her chin, and a bit on the messy side. She was dressed simply, in a gray sweater and black slacks. I guessed her age to be somewhere in her fifties. It was hard to tell exactly. I've never been too good at guessing how old adults are.

"I'm Mallory Pike," I said, sure that my

name would be familiar to her after three letters.

An amused smile formed on Ms. Hayes's lips. I hoped I hadn't sounded stupid. "How can I help you, Mallory?"

"Didn't you get my letters?" I blurted out.

Ms. Hayes looked at me, and her expression didn't reveal anything.

She thinks I'm a maniac, I told myself, losing hope. My idol now thinks I'm a complete nut case. I've ruined everything.

"I can't say I remember your letters at this very moment." Henrietta Hayes spoke slowly. "But since you're here, why don't you come in?"

My tight, anxious shoulders relaxed. I should have known it took more than one awkward eleven-year-old fan to unnerve the author of *Alice Anderson*. "Thank you," I said as graciously as I could manage. I picked my notebook up off the ground, fumbled my questionnaire back into my pack, and stepped inside the home of the world's greatest living author. (The greatest in my opinion, anyway.)

I liked her simply furnished home. The couch and chairs were wood-framed with cushions in deep, rusty shades of brown, gold, and red. On her golden brown walls hung large works of art. Some were prints by artists

I recognized, such as Van Gogh and Renoir. Others were original paintings and sketches by artists I didn't know.

"Would you like some tea?" Ms. Hayes offered.

"No, thanks," I said, not wanting to be a bother.

"Some hot chocolate then?"

I didn't want to be rude, either, so I agreed. "That would be nice, if it's not too much trouble."

"No trouble," said Ms. Hayes. She left the living room and went into her kitchen, across the hall. I wasn't sure if I should follow her or stay put. I took a chance and followed her into a country kitchen with white cabinets and a yellow and white tile floor.

A large picture window looked out onto her yard. Gazing out the window, I saw she had a flower garden, though most of it was now turning brown. Only a patch of orange and yellow chrysanthemums still bloomed.

"So, what brings you to my door?" asked Ms. Hayes as she put a bright blue tea kettle on the stove. Somehow it seemed so right that Henrietta Hayes wouldn't own a microwave oven, which is what we use to make hot water in our house.

"Well, I wrote you some letters about it," I began. "I know you received them, because

60

I got replies from you, but . . ." I stopped, because I didn't want to sound as if I were complaining — even though I *was* complaining.

"But you got a form letter back," Ms. Hayes said sadly.

"Well, yes."

"I feel so bad about those letters, but I'll tell you, Mallory, mail became quite a dilemma for me. I used to try to answer all my letters personally, and as a result a great many letters went unanswered. There were simply too many. Answering them all took up every bit of my time. So, after a while I started putting them aside for a moment when I would have some time, and that time never came. I'd feel terribly guilty. When I finally said, I must answer these this minute, I'd look at them and find that some were nearly a year old. I felt foolish writing things like, 'You may remember that you wrote me almost a year ago. . . .' I had to come up with a solution, and that solution was the form letter."

"That makes sense," I said.

"I can imagine how unsatisfying it must be to receive a reply like that," Ms. Hayes went on, taking lovely pink teacups from her cabinets. "Yet it's better than being ignored, don't you think?"

"Oh, yes," I agreed. "That would be worse."

"Of course it would," said Ms. Hayes. "So, now tell me what you wrote to me."

"I guess that means you didn't read my letter," I said. "I thought maybe you hadn't."

"I would have read it eventually," Ms. Hayes assured me as she set out the cups. "But I can't guarantee when. See those?" She nodded to a willow basket filled with blank stamped envelopes which sat on a table in the corner. "The moment a letter comes in, I look at its return address. I write the address on one of those envelopes — each one has a form letter inside — and put it right into the mail. After that, I set the letter aside to read when I can. I do treasure the letters. They mean so much. They're very encouraging."

"Good thing I came here, then," I said. "By the time you read my letter it would have been too late."

"Too late for what?" Ms. Hayes asked.

"For my report." I told her every detail of what had happened: from my discovering her books, to Mr. Williams' rejecting my proposal, to my coming up with the brilliant idea of improving the project by including her in it, and then to my being inspired by Alice Anderson to come to her house myself.

Ms. Hayes clapped her hands with delight at the last part. "So Alice inspired you, did she? How wonderful. You don't know, Mallory, how happy that makes me. That's exactly what I wanted Alice to do — inspire girls to take life head on, and not let anything get in their way. Oh, you have really made my day. Thank you, Mallory."

"You're welcome," I said. "Thank you for writing about Alice."

Ms. Hayes smiled just as the kettle let off a high pitched whistle. "Let's get going on that project of yours," she said gamely, shutting off the flame and pouring water into our cups.

"Are you sure you have time?" I asked.

Ms. Hayes laughed, as she stirred in the hot chocolate mix. "Would Alice have asked that?"

"No, I guess not. Okay. Here's my first question . . ." As I went down my list, Ms. Hayes answered every question. I learned that she wrote for four hours every day. Then she spent two more hours working on outlines for new projects.

"That, to me, is the hardest part," she admitted. "I find the writing fairly easy. Ideas are often more difficult to come by."

She told me that her ideas came from life combined with imagination. "Sometimes I put real people I've observed into situations I've created with my imagination," she explained.

I longed to ask her if she was Alice or Alice's mother. Somehow, though, sitting there face-to-face, it seemed like too nosy a question.

Instead, I stayed with easier questions such as, "How did you feel when you saw your first play performed?"

"Terrible," Ms. Hayes admitted. (I'd expected her to say she felt great.) "It wasn't nearly as terrific as I'd thought it was when I'd finished writing."

"That was 'Vacation at Frog Pond'?"

"Yes! You've really done your homework, Mallory."

"I know all the titles of your books and plays," I told her. "I'm not finished with the entire 'Alice Anderson' series yet but pretty soon I'll be finished. Are you working on something new?"

"Always," Ms. Hayes said with a smile. She tapped her forehead. "I can't seem to turn this thing off."

"I hope it's another Alice book," I said.

"No, it's not," Ms. Hayes said, sipping her hot chocolate. "You'd like to see another, would you?"

"Very much," I said. "I can't stand the idea of never finding out what happens to Alice, you know, in her life and all."

Ms. Hayes looked at me in the same blank way she had when she'd met me in the doorway. "You may have given me an idea," she said after a moment.

"What?" I asked.

Ms. Hayes waved her finger. "No, no. I never talk about my ideas until they're on paper. Talking about them has a way of making them die out on me. I'm not sure why."

"All right, then don't tell me," I said quickly. I went on and finished my questions. I scribbled Ms. Hayes's replies down so fast my hand hurt after awhile. "Thank you so much, Ms. Hayes," I said when I had asked my last question. "I really, really appreciate this."

"You're welcome, Mallory," said Ms. Hayes, frowning.

"Is something wrong?" I asked.

"No, it's just that I'm not sure I've given you a good sense of what the life of an author is really like," she said.

"I do have a lot more questions if you ever have any more time to spare," I dared to say. "I mean, I'm sure I could think of a lot more questions. There's so much I'd like to know."

"You know, Mallory, I have an idea. How would you like to earn a little money?"

"I already do — I mean, I baby-sit — but what were you thinking?" I asked as I stood up.

"I'm in the middle of two big projects right now. I could use an assistant around here for the next three weeks. It wouldn't be too hard — filing, a little typing, maybe making some phone calls for me. Then you could see for yourself what my workday is like. Would you be interested?"

"Oh, Ms. Hayes," I gasped. "I am so interested you wouldn't believe it! Yes! Yes! Absolutely!"

I felt so overwhelmed I had to lean on a kitchen chair a moment for support. I would be working for my favorite author. This had to be a dream. But it wasn't!

Up until now I knew I wanted to be an author, but I really had no idea how I'd get my books published. By working as Ms. Hayes's assistant I'd learn how it was done. And I'd be able to ask Ms. Hayes questions. She could give me advice about how to improve my work and who to send it to. This was a giant step forward on the road toward becoming a real author.

"This is terrific, Mallory," said Ms. Hayes. "I needed an assistant, and here you are. It's as if fate brought you here."

Fate! What an author-like thing to say.

She was right, though. It was fate.

At that moment I had the sense that my life was about to change — forever.

CHAPTER 7

The very next afternoon I reported for my first day as Ms. Hayes's assistant. "Here's where I work," she said, showing me a small room with a very large wooden desk, on which sat an electric typewriter.

"You don't use a computer?" I asked.

"Oh, I know I should," Ms. Hayes said with a laugh, stepping into the room. "But I can't quite deal with the idea. To me, this typewriter seems like high technology. I bought it only last year and I still can't believe how amazing it is. I can read two sentences on this print display here and change them as much as I like before printing."

I nodded and decided that when I knew Ms. Hayes better I would offer to teach her how to use a computer word processing program. Mom showed me how and it's not that hard.

Bookshelves lined the back wall of the office from floor to ceiling. The top three shelves were all books by Henrietta Hayes. "That's where I keep my author's copies of my own work," Ms. Hayes explained, when she saw me staring at the books. "The next three shelves contain books written by friends of mine, and below that are books I love to reread from time to time."

"Wow! You know Amelia Moody!" I exclaimed, noticing her copy of *Nitty Gritty Meatballs* on the fifth shelf down.

"Amelia is a dear friend of mine," said Ms. Hayes. "She visited me just last week."

"Gosh," I murmured. I wondered how many other wonderful, famous authors would be dropping by to visit Ms. Hayes. Maybe I would be here when they dropped by. The thought of it gave me goosebumps.

Next to Ms. Hayes's desk was a very large willow basket cluttered with official-looking papers and fat typewritten manuscripts. Ms. Hayes picked it up. "This is the first thing I'll need you to do," she said. "These desperately need to be filed. I can't cram another thing into this office so I keep the filing cabinets in a different room. Come with me."

I followed Ms. Hayes back out into the hall. We went down three brown-carpeted stairs to a large room with a stone fireplace. The sliding glass doors set in the far wall looked out onto the woods. A long wooden table stood not far from the door. Behind it were three wooden filing cabinets. Ms. Hayes set the basket on the table.

"The best way for you to proceed, Mallory, will be to make piles here on the table. Sort everything by project title, which you'll almost always find somewhere on the paper. If you can't tell where something belongs, put it in a 'Don't Know' pile and I'll look at it later. If the phone rings, please answer it and take a message. Or let my machine pick it up. I don't speak to anyone during my writing time."

As she spoke, I noticed a small room off the family room we were in. The door was ajar and I could see in. It appeared to be a girl's bedroom. Pink ruffled curtains hung on the window. They matched the pink bedspread on the twin bed. "Is that your daughter's room?" I asked.

Ms. Hayes's pale skin took on an almost gray color. "My daughter?"

"That just looks like a girl's room so I thought . . ."

Ms. Hayes whirled around toward the door. She stared into the room for a moment, then pulled the door shut firmly. "The cleaning lady must have left that open," she said, annoyed.

"I didn't mean to be nosy or anything," I began, my voice coming out all trembly.

"No, it's all right. It's fine," Ms. Hayes said sharply. She took a few breaths to compose herself. "I apologize if I seem agitated. Yes, that room belonged to my daughter, Cassie. She's dead now."

Dead! I had that same feeling you get when someone hits you hard in the chest with a snowball that you didn't even see coming. It's a combination of shock, hurt, and anger. I was angry at myself for opening my big mouth. "I'm so sorry, Ms. Hayes," I said.

Ms. Hayes waved her hand briskly as if to make the subject go away. "Thank you. But I'd rather not talk about it. It's too . . . I just never do talk about it."

"Sure," I said.

"At any rate, this filing should take you about two hours, I would think. When you're done, please come and get me in my office."

"All right," I agreed.

After Ms. Hayes left, the room suddenly seemed extremely quiet. In my house, quiet is something you never hear. Even at night the refrigerator hums, the old hall clock ticks, and occasionally a car passes on the street. There are always doors opening and shutting as someone makes a trip to the bathroom or to the kitchen. But at that moment, there in

Henrietta Hayes's home, there was complete, absolute silence.

Which was why I almost jumped out of my sneakers when the phone rang. I leaped to answer it, not wanting Ms. Hayes to be disturbed.

"Hello, is Henrietta there?" a man on the other end asked.

"No . . . um . . . this is . . . um . . . her assistant . . . her new assistant, Mallory. Can I take a message? Ms. Hayes doesn't wish to be disturbed right now."

"Oh, right, I forgot," said the man. "I usually get her answering machine at this time. Well, tell Henrietta that George Delmore called, and I love her idea for an Anderson Family reunion book. Tell her I want to talk to her about it as soon as possible."

"Oh, my gosh! You're doing an Anderson family reunion!" I cried happily. "That is so great!"

"Yes, we thought it was a good idea," George Delmore said.

"It is, it's a great idea," I agreed. "I'll tell Ms. Hayes you called."

"Yes, please do. Tell her we're all very excited about it and we're going to want this fast."

"I'll tell her. 'Bye." When I hung up, I was

so excited I completely forgot what Ms. Hayes had said about not wanting to be disturbed. I ran out of the room, up the steps, and down the hall. "Ms. Hayes," I said excitedly, bursting into her office.

Ms. Hayes sat there with a framed picture in her hands. My eyes darted to the picture. It showed a pretty teenaged girl with long brown hair and large brown eyes. Ms. Hayes put the picture down quickly on her lap. "Yes, Mallory?"

"Oh, I'm so sorry to bother you. I forgot . . . I . . ."

"That's all right. What is it?"

I told her what George Delmore had said. Ms. Hayes smiled. "That was the inspiration you gave me yesterday. I knew George would like it. It's a good idea. Now, Mallory, we'll have to come up with some thoughts about what happened to Alice for the rest of her life. Did she marry? Become a movie star? And what about Lars and the rest? If you have any ideas let me know. George wants everything fast."

"Yes, he said that," I recalled.

"He always does," Ms. Hayes laughed. "So, I'm serious about being open to any suggestions you'd care to offer. I don't want to steal your ideas, of course, so only give them if you don't mind my using them."

"Mind?" I cried. "It would be an honor. That's all I'll be thinking about. Alice Anderson is so real to me I feel as if I'd be influencing the life of a real person."

"It does feel that way sometimes," Ms. Hayes agreed with a smile. "Characters have a peculiar way of taking on lives of their own. It's a strange, almost magical process. After awhile, an author becomes as fond of her characters as if they were real friends."

"But the characters really are real, so they do have a life of their own," I said.

"In a way," replied Ms. Hayes.

"Well, I'd better get back to work," I said, backing out of the study. Ms. Hayes had been right. It took me about two hours to finish the filing. She appeared in the doorway just as I slipped a letter to her editor into the correct file.

"It's starting to get dark so early," she said. "I insist you take a cab home."

"I have my bike," I reminded her.

"The driver can put it in the trunk. Would you care to join me for supper? I've made my special beef stew tonight."

"I'd love to," I said. "Can I call home?"

"Of course."

Mom said it was all right for me to stay since I'd be driven home. Ms. Hayes had made a delicious stew. I wondered where her husband was. I figure I'd asked enough nosy questions for one day, though. As we ate, we discussed things that might have happened to Alice. I hadn't quite finished *Alice Anderson's Greatest Challenge* yet. I was up to the part where Alice gets a great role in a movie, but on the same day she receives a letter from Lars saying that their mother is sick. "Does Alice stay in Hollywood or go home?" I asked Ms. Hayes.

Ms. Hayes broke off a piece of bread and laughed. "I'm not going to spoil the end of the book for you. We'll talk more after you finish it."

That evening, I felt very special as I was driven down Slate Street in a cab. As I climbed out, I looked around quickly, hoping people were watching me and wondering what Mallory Pike was doing arriving in a cab. I'd only worked for Henrietta Hayes one day, and already I felt like a different person — a more important, more talented, and intelligent person.

In the house, Dad and Jordan were at the kitchen table going over Jordan's math homework. From the sound of it (a sound sort of like a buffalo stampede) everyone else was downstairs in the rec room. "How did it go?" Dad asked as I came in.

"Words can not describe the greatness of being Henrietta Hayes's assistant," I said seriously. "I've already given her a book idea."

"Good for you," said Dad. "This might turn out to be an important job for you."

"Maybe," I agreed, although that wasn't the most important thing to me right then. It was wonderful enough just to know Ms. Hayes and have the chance to talk to her.

I was so inspired that I went right upstairs to work on my own play. I'd entitled it, "The Early Years." It was the story of a young author in the early years of her life. Of course, the young author was me, but I'd fictionalized the story a little so no one would be offended.

Lying on my bed, I read over what I'd already written, which wasn't much more than the opening. Here's what it said.

Valery Spike sits at her writing table and looks out her window longingly.
Valery: How I wish I could write something truly great, something that would change the world and make people happy, especially children.
Enter Ranessa. Klutzy Ranessa trips over a chair as she enters.
Ranessa: Ouch! Ow! Who put that chair there?
Valery (Kindly): Why, it's always been there, Ranessa.
Ranessa (with envy in her voice): It's no fair, Valery. In this family you got the looks, the brains, the talent. It's just not fair.

Valery (sighing): There's one thing I don't have—
privacy. How can I ever hope to be a great
writer in this family? Every two seconds
there's another interruption.

Enter Ricky, with a bucket stuck on his head.

Ricky: Help! Help! I'm stuck.

Ranessa tries to help him but she falls over
the chair again and knocks him down. They
both roll on the ground.

Margarita enters, twirling a Skip-It over her
head.

Margarita: Yippee-iii-kay-yah. I can't skip
over this, but I sure am going to use it for something.
It's a great lasso.

As Ricky gets up with the bucket still on his
head, Margarita's Skip-It bangs into the bucket.
With a loud clang, Ricky falls down again.

Mrs. Spike enters.

Mrs. Spike: Valery dear, I want you to baby-sit
for your brothers and sisters, and scrub the
floors, and take out the garbage. Could you
also patch that hole in the livingroom wall?
Okay, dear?

Valery: All right, Mother dear. With all these
children, I know you need the help.

Valery gets up from her desk and pulls the bucket
off of Ricky's head. Sighs deeply.

Valery: My family needs me desperately, so the
world will have to wait to read the stories
which I hope some day to write.

When I finished reading it, I felt pleased. It had comedy (the bucket stuff and all), and tragedy (the poor writer burdened with an insensitive, needy family), and it was taken from my true life experiences.

Filled with quiet excitement, I clicked my ballpoint pen and began writing the further adventures of the maniac Spike family.

CHAPTER 8

The kids in the KCDAC are really
excited about Mallory's play. It was
fun going to the meeting with her
today. I'm a little worried about
the play, though, Mal. How will your
brothers and sisters feel when they
see it? I don't think they'll be
too thrilled.

Stacey helped me pass out the copies of my completed play to the kids in the KCDAC. I figured they were ready to work on it. Last week I'd assigned them to do improvisations. That's when you describe a situation and ask the kids to act it out using their own words. (I'd read about improvising in *The Basics of Play Writing*. The kids did well with it, so now they were ready to start my play.)

"All right, everybody," I said. "Take a few minutes to read this over, and then we'll read some scenes. Stacey and I will decide who we think should act out which part. Okay?"

The kids nodded and began reading. Haley giggled from time to time, but Becca frowned deeply. "Is Ranessa supposed to be Vanessa?" she asked finally.

"Umm . . . I just changed that character's name," I said, avoiding the question. "From now on she's named . . . Jill." Ranessa was a little too close to Vanessa.

"It's Vanessa," Haley said knowingly to Becca.

"Is this play about your family?" Stacey asked me.

"Well, yes," I admitted. "All great literature is basically autobiographical."

Stacey wrinkled her nose thoughtfully. "Are

you sure? What about, say, *Peter Pan*?"

"J.M. Barrie isn't considered one of the world's great writers," I replied.

"What about, oh, *Stuart Little* or *Charlotte's Web*?" Stacey continued.

"Okay, they're fantasies," I said. "It's hard to tell what parts of E.B. White's life are in those. But I bet if I knew more about his life I could find things that were the same. After all, Stuart Little lives in an apartment in Manhattan."

"I know," Stacey said, a fond look coming into her blue eyes. "That's one of the things I always loved best about that book. Plus, after I read *Stuart Little* I never thought about mice the same way again. Whenever anyone caught a mouse in a trap, I felt sad, like it might be Stuart Little."

"Exactly," I said, although her remark didn't prove my point at all. Maybe little kids' books aren't autobiographical, but books for older kids are. "Take *Little Women*," I said. "Louisa May Alcott really did have sisters, and she did live in the North during the Civil War."

We didn't have time to discuss it further because the kids started to look restless. "Well, what do you think of the play?" I asked them.

"It's pretty funny," said the girl I didn't know. Her name was Wendy.

"Is it a comedy?" Stacey asked me in a low voice.

"Parts of it are," I said. "All right, let's start reading. Becca, you read Valery's part. Haley, you be Ranessa, I mean Jill. Tony, you read Ricky's part. And Danielle, you be Margarita."

"Where should we start?" asked Becca.

"Try the final scene, where Valery is sick in bed." I'd written this scene thinking about the time I'd been sick with mononucleosis. I'd missed tons of school, and wasn't even allowed to baby-sit for awhile.

"Should we stand or sit?" asked Haley.

"I think they should stand," Stacey suggested to me.

"Yes, stand," I agreed. "You guys will have to get used to talking on your feet. Take it from Valery's line, 'I'm all right. I want to know how I can help *you*.'"

The kids stood in the center of the circle of chairs. Becca read Valery's first line.

"Oh, you're so unselfish, Valery," said Danielle, as Margarita.

"I care about my family," read Becca.

"But you're so sick, Valery," said Danielle.

"It's true, my play is unfinished, but you all need me so much," Becca read. "I'm not too sick to help my family."

Stacey volunteered to read the mother's part. (After the meeting she told me that she enjoyed it. It reminded her of when she played Mrs. Darling in *Peter Pan*.)

"Oh, Valery," Stacey read. "I blame myself. I worked you too hard.

"No, Mother, don't blame yourself," Becca said. "It's my fault. I stayed up late trying to do my writing. I exhausted myself."

"Valery, when you're better, we'll make sure you have time for your writing," said Haley.

"Forget it," said Tony, as Ricky. "Valery gets all the attention. That's not fair."

"Okay, thanks," I stopped them. I'd seen enough. They were all pretty bad — all except Danielle. She read her lines with some expression, not like a robot. "I realize this is the first time you guys have seen the script," I said. "But try to put a little more feeling into it."

For the next reading, Stacey suggested having Danielle read Valery's part. I agreed. We read another section of the play, one with the Jordan, Byron, and Adam characters in it. Of course, I'd changed their names. Bruce read Myron, Buddy Barrett read Atlas, and a boy named Peter Tiegreen read Gordon. I asked Charlotte to read the part of Delaware, who was based on Claire.

"But this is a baby's part," Charlotte objected.

"A great actress can play anything," I insisted.

"I don't want this part," Charlotte said firmly. "I'm not playing a five-year-old. And I'm certainly not a great actress. I want to work on the costumes."

I ignored the last part of Charlotte's comment. "All right. I just changed Delaware to a six-year-old."

"But she still sounds like a baby."

"Well, I'll rewrite that character, I suppose," I grumbled. "Turn to the next page and read the Jill part."

In this scene, Valery finally finishes her great play, only to have Myron, Gordon, and Atlas use it to build a fire. (This never happened to me, but it was the kind of thing the triplets might easily do.)

"My play! Oh, no! What have you done with my play?" Danielle read dramatically.

"What play?" asked Peter.

"That's my play you just threw in the fire!" cried Danielle.

"That big bunch of papers?" read Buddy. "We thought it was garbage."

"No! No!" Danielle sobbed. "That was my play, the one I've been trying to write all year."

"You've burned Valery's play!" said Charlotte in a mechanical voice I had to strain to hear.

"Relax, would you?" Bruce read. "She can always write another one."

"Not bad," I told them. "Danielle, you were terrific."

"Thanks," she said with a sweet smile.

We asked the kids to run through a few more scenes. By the time we were done, it was clear that Danielle was the best actress in the group. Stacey and I told the kids to take a break while we discussed who should play which role.

"We know Danielle will play you . . . I mean, Valery," said Stacey.

"I'm worried about her being sick, though," I said quietly. "Becca told Jessi she's started missing a lot of school because of her doctor appointments. What if she misses rehearsals, or even misses the play itself?"

"Who else could handle that part?" Stacey asked.

No one could. "We'll just have to take a chance with Danielle, I suppose," I agreed. "We can make someone her understudy."

"Good idea," Stacey agreed.

In the end we cast Danielle as Valery, Bruce as Myron, Peter as Atlas, Buddy as Gordon, Wendy as Margarita, Haley as Jill, Sara as the now six-year-old Delaware as well as Danielle's understudy, and Tony as Ricky. Becca would play Valery's best friend Sissy. Char would play the mother. The mother didn't say much, so Char would be easy to replace, in case her stage fright kicked up.

"Memorize your lines," I told the kids just before the meeting ended. "I'd like to start working without scripts as soon as we can."

On the way home, Stacey was quiet. "What are you thinking?" I asked.

"I'm wondering what your family will think when they see that play," she said. "Don't you think they'll be insulted? It *is* a little exaggerated."

"If I didn't exaggerate a little, it wouldn't be interesting," I said. "It's called dramatization."

"Won't they be mad when they finally read it?"

"I won't show it to them."

Stacey laughed. "Haley has already figured out that it's about you and your family. Don't you think she might tell Vanessa?"

"I guess," I admitted. "But what am I supposed to do? If I can't use my life and the people in it, how can I write anything?"

"Write about other people," Stacey suggested.

I threw my arms up. "Then it wouldn't be honest writing. It would be a big lie."

"I don't know about that," said Stacey. "But

it's up to you, anyway. Just be prepared for trouble."

I pressed my lips together thoughtfully. This was a real dilemma. Maybe Ms. Hayes could advise me. Then again, maybe she couldn't. After all, if she'd drawn on her family life in order to write her books — and I was sure she had — she wouldn't have a problem like this. I mean, if your family is funny, kind-hearted, and happy, and you write about them, who's going to complain? But a writer has to draw from the raw material he or she has been given, and, like it or not, I was stuck with the Spike family.

CHAPTER 9

"This sounds terrific so far, Mallory. What have you learned about Ms. Hayes from your other sources?" Mr. Williams asked me that Friday in class. He had allotted five minutes with each student, to see how our projects were coming along.

"What do you mean?" I asked. "What other sources?"

"Aren't you consulting other sources about the life of Henrietta Hayes?"

"Why?" I asked. "I have the main source herself right in front of me. What could be better than that?" I'd seen Ms. Hayes just the day before and interviewed her again. We talked about her days at Ithaca College. Back then she'd enrolled in the theater department, wanting to be an actress (just like Alice Anderson), but when she discovered she could never find roles she wanted to play, she began writing her own. Soon she found she liked writing better than acting.

"I'd like to see some biographical data from other sources," Mr. Williams said. "Magazines, biographies, newspaper clippings. You might learn a lot more about Ms. Hayes than you'd expect. People don't always tell you everything about themselves. A good researcher does her background homework, too."

"All right," I agreed.

At first, it seemed like a big waste of time to me. But when I thought about it some more, maybe Mr. Williams had a point. There were some questions that seemed too personal to ask Ms. Hayes. Anytime I tried a family question, Ms. Hayes started talking about something else. I couldn't tell if she wanted to avoid the subject, or if she'd truly become distracted. I noticed that her mind did sometimes jump around from subject to subject, in what seemed like a haphazard way.

After school that afternoon, I set out for the Stoneybrook Public Library. As soon as I walked in, I spotted Mrs. Kishi, Claudia's mom. She's the head librarian.

Waving to her, I headed over to the Guide to Periodical Literature section. The guides are a bunch of books which list all the recent magazine and newspaper articles which have been written on different people and subjects. I pulled out the most recent one and thumbed through to the H section, looking for Henrietta Hayes.

"Hello, Mallory," said Mrs. Kishi, as she returned two thick reference books to the shelf. "What are you working on?"

"I have to write a report on Henrietta Hayes," I explained.

"Oh, the author. Her work is wonderful. She lives right here in Stoneybrook, you know," said Mrs. Kishi.

"I know that," I replied excitedly. "But how did *you* know?"

"Librarians have ways of finding these things out," Mrs. Kishi said with a smile. "I have files on all our local authors."

"You mean there are others?" I cried.

"A few. I think Henrietta Hayes is the only juvenile author, although there are a few picture book illustrators in town."

"Wow!" I said. I had no idea!

"Would you like to see the file on Henrietta Hayes?" Mrs. Kishi offered.

"That would be great," I said, closing the guide. I followed Mrs. Kishi into the office behind the main checkout desk. Black metal file cabinets stood side by side against the back wall. She pulled open the top drawer of one of them. "Hayes . . . Hayes . . . Hayes . . ." she repeated softly as she searched for the correct folder. "Here we are. Hayes, Henrietta."

Mrs. Kishi handed me the well-stuffed manila folder. "This should give you plenty to look at. I can't let you check this out, but you know where the copier is, don't you?"

"Over to the right," I said. "That's a good idea. I'll copy whatever I can't read today. Thanks, Mrs. Kishi."

Feeling as if I'd just discovered buried treasure, I hurried over to a couch in the corner of the library. Mrs. Kishi had just saved me hours of work.

The first three articles I read through didn't tell me anything I didn't already know about Ms. Hayes. Then I came across a real find — a five page article clipped from *People* magazine. The date on it was from last year. The article was entitled: "Henrietta Hayes: The Happiest Writer," which, I suppose, was a takeoff on her play, "The Happiest Day." On the first page I learned that an Alice Anderson TV movie was being planned. I must have missed it. I'd have to ask Ms. Hayes about it. Maybe it would be out on video soon.

The article had lots to say about Ms. Hayes's

early career. I began scribbling down notes like crazy — all sorts of exact dates, names, and places that I'd been careless about taking down when I interviewed Ms. Hayes. Mr. Williams would want that kind of information, I was sure.

Toward the middle of the article, I stopped writing. I put my pen down and stared at the paper in my hands. I couldn't quite believe what the article had to say.

Henrietta Hayes's personal history stands in stark contrast to the sunny optimism of her books. A foster child from the age of three, when her parents and younger brother died tragically in a fire, Ms. Hayes never knew the tight family bonds that figure so prominently in virtually all of her fiction. The first time she lived in one place for more than a year was when she attended Ithaca College on a theater department scholarship. Even as an adult, her marriage to author G.N. Rogers ended in bitter divorce resulting in a fierce and prolonged custody battle over their only child, Cassandra. Ms. Hayes finally won full custody of Cassandra, whom she called Cassie. Sadly, Cassie was to die a mere three years later, at the age of eighteen, the victim of a hit-and-run driver. Despite her history of personal tragedy, Ms. Hayes presents to her readers a world in which things turn out for the best and . . .

I felt too shocked to read on. I put the article down and gazed blankly at the bookshelf in front of me. This had to be some big mistake. The article couldn't possibly be about the same person who wrote, *The Happiest Day*, *Vacation at Frog Pond*, *Ain't Life Grand*, and all the Alice Anderson books. There had to be some explanation.

In a daze, I photocopied the rest of the magazine articles to read at home. Then I went back to the periodical guide and looked up G.N. Rogers. There were a lot of articles on Ms. Hayes's ex-husband, even though I'd never heard of him.

The articles I found made G.N. Rogers sound like a pretty unpleasant person. His books were described as "dark and forbidding," or as "presenting a world of hopelessness." His photo showed a frowning man with deep, worried creases on his broad forehead. There was even an article about his divorce from Ms. Hayes, which showed him shouting at her outside a courtroom.

Next, I looked up Cassandra Rogers in the periodical guide, but didn't find anything about her.

"Are you feeling all right, Mallory?" asked Mrs. Kishi, coming over to where I sat on the couch, with the periodical guide in my lap.

"You look pale. Would you like me to call your parents? I know you've been ill."

"Oh, no thanks," I replied, snapping out of my shocked daze. "I'm fine. I think I just need some air or something."

"Are you sure?" Mrs. Kishi asked.

"Yes, I'm okay," I said, closing the guide and getting up. "Thanks again for the file. Want me to bring it to the front desk?"

"No, that's all right. You're welcome," said Mrs. Kishi, taking the file from me.

Still a bit stunned, I made my way out of the library. What would Ernest Hemingway think of Ms. Hayes? Her writing wasn't autobiographical at all. How could she write about happy, close-knit families when she'd never had one, not even as a child? And if she didn't know what she was talking about, then it was all lies.

Wasn't it?

But how could her books be filled with lies? They didn't seem that way. They seemed honest and full of true feelings. They'd made me laugh and cry.

It was so confusing. I loved Ms. Hayes's books. Yet, if a good writer had to draw on her life experiences, was Ms. Hayes really a good writer? Maybe I was wrong about her. Maybe she wasn't such a good writer.

A cold wind whipped brown oak leaves around me. The late-afternoon sky had turned gray. I headed home with my hands jammed in my pockets, wondering how this new information would affect my English project, and what I'd say to Henrietta Hayes the next time I went to her house.

CHAPTER 10

monday

Mallory, no offense, but you're out of your mind. How could you write that play? You must have known your family would get mad. What were you thinking? Now you have some mess to deal with. Good luck on this one.

That next Monday, Kristy volunteered to help me with my first Kids Club rehearsal of *The Early Years*. Ms. Simon had arranged for us to use the stage in the auditorium. I was happy about that because I wanted the kids to feel comfortable on stage right from the start.

When Kristy arrived, Charlotte Johanssen was already onstage, about to start reading the part of Mrs Spike.

"Where's Danielle?" Kristy asked, looking around.

"I don't know. She must've been sick, or had a doctor's appointment. She's really a good actress, but I was afraid this would happen," I replied.

Kristy frowned and nodded. She's a perfectionist herself and sympathized with my problem.

"All right, Charlotte," I called up to the stage. "Take it from 'Oh, Valery. I blame myself.'"

Charlotte stepped into the middle of the stage, holding her script. "Oh, Valery. I blame myself. I worked you too hard," she said in a timid voice.

"Louder," I interrupted her from my seat beside Kristy in the front row of the auditorium.

Charlotte nodded and went back to her script. This time, as she spoke the words, her voice gradually grew lower, and lower, and lower. "Speak up, Char," I said.

"I am speaking up," Charlotte replied quietly.

Kristy couldn't resist the urge to take charge for a moment longer. "Just talk a little louder than your usual voice," she said, standing up in front of her seat. "Talk like this," she added, raising her voice but not shouting.

Char nodded again and went back to reading the play. Very quietly.

I sighed.

Haley, as Jill, came on next. She flapped her arms like an alarmed bird. "Where's the chair I'm supposed to fall over?"

"Don't worry about it," I told her. "I've changed your character a little. She's not a klutz anymore. She talks in rhymes all the time instead." I'd decided Vanessa wasn't really clumsy as much as sort of spacey sometimes, especially when she had her mind on a poem.

"I practiced falling all day yesterday," Haley complained. "I had it just right, too."

"Sorry," I told her. "I'll have new scripts for everybody by next week. Why don't we skip to where Ricky comes in with the bucket stuck on his head."

"I don't have a bucket," said Tony, walking out on stage.

"Pretend," said Kristy.

"Yeah, pretend," I said.

Tony closed his eyes and staggered around the stage with his arms out. He crashed into Haley. "Hey, watch it," Haley complained.

"How can I watch it when I have a bucket over my head?" Tony asked.

"Just say your lines, you guys," Kristy called to them. She looked at me, her eyes wide with exasperation. She was probably thinking that if *she* were in charge things wouldn't be so chaotic. (And I'm sure that's true.)

"Help! Help! I'm stuck!" cried Tony.

Haley mimed pulling the bucket from his head. Abruptly, she stopped and turned to me. "Do we fall over if I'm not a klutz any-more?" she asked.

"Uh . . . yeah. You can still fall over," I replied.

Charlotte and Tony fell backward onto the stage. Charlotte tumbled over with them. "You're not supposed to fall, Char," I said.

"I couldn't help it, they knocked me down," Charlotte grumbled. "Be more careful, would you?" she scolded Haley and Ricky.

"Do I come on now?" asked Wendy, sticking her head out from behind the side curtains.

"Yes!" Kristy and I called back at the same

time. Kristy couldn't stand much more of this confusion. She's so orderly it was driving her crazy. I'm sure she couldn't believe I'd let things get this disorganized, but change is part of being creative. Right now the kids were adjusting to all the changes I'd made in my play.

Wendy skipped out, twirling the Skip-It over her head. "Yabba-dabba-dooooo!" she shouted.

"It's Yippeee-iii-kay-yah!" Kristy corrected her, pointing to the line in the script.

"I know, but I thought Yabba-dabba-doooo would be funnier since this is a comedy and — "

Before Wendy could say more, Kristy turned toward the back of the auditorium. Vanessa, Margo, Byron, Adam, Jordan, and Nicky marched angrily down the center aisle. "I told you! See? That nut with the Skip-It is supposed to be you, Margo!" said Vanessa.

"You're in trouble now," Kristy said as she turned back toward me.

"What are you guys doing here?" I demanded.

"We heard from a reliable source that you are deflaming our characters," Vanessa said angrily.

"That word is defaming," Kristy corrected her.

"Whatever it is, we hate it!" Margo shouted. "I don't go around twirling Skip-Its over my head."

"And I'm not a klutz," added Vanessa.

"I'm changing that part," I said weakly.

"You made me look like a jerk," Nicky complained. "I never, ever got a bucket stuck on my head."

"Then how do you know that's supposed to be you?" I challenged them. "How do any of you know?"

"Oh, like, *duh*, Mallory, you went and changed my name from Byron to Myron. That really makes it hard to figure out."

"How did you know about that?" I asked Byron.

Vanessa waved a copy of my play in the air. "We read this!"

"Who gave it to you?"

"That's not important," said Vanessa, which was a good clue that it was either Haley, Charlotte, or Becca. "The important thing is that we want you to stop this play right now."

"I can't, Vanessa. This is the play I wrote."

"I wish we *had* burned it," Adam said sulkily. "That's the only good scene in the whole stupid play."

"If you put this play on, everyone will laugh at us," said Margo.

"Yeah, they'll think we're a bunch of real losers," said Byron.

"You're not losers," I said. "But this is the story of my life."

"Oh, yeah, like you're such a perfect saint," Jordan scoffed.

By now, all the Kids Club actors had gathered at the edge of the stage to listen. Kristy pulled herself up onto the stage. "Come on, you guys. I think you're all a little stiff," she told them. "Let's do some jumping jacks."

"Jumping jacks?" Char complained.

"Yeah, that's just what all of you need. Jumping jacks."

As the stage behind me thundered with the sound of jumping, I stared into the glaring eyes of my brothers and sisters. "I can make little changes," I told them. "I'm still making small corrections here and there. I can't change you guys altogether, your characters, I mean. Otherwise it wouldn't be coming from my true experience. An author's work must be autobiographical."

"That bucket thing isn't true," Nicky argued.

"No, but you're always getting stuck in stuff. You got your head stuck in the banister once, and you got stuck in the clothes hamper. Do you remember that?" I shot back.

"But not a bucket," said Nicky, folding his arms stubbornly.

"The bucket is just a way of showing all those times rolled into one." I defended my work. "You *are the sort* of character who gets stuck in weird stuff!"

"We may seem like these characters to your sick mind," said Vanessa in a voice so anger-filled that it shook. "But it isn't how we are. I'm going to write a poem called 'Seven Sweet Kids and Their Lying, Selfish, Stuck-Up Oldest Sister.' And I'm going to have it printed in the school paper. See how you like that!"

"Vanessa," I pleaded. "Try to understand."

Vanessa was now red-faced with fury. "If you put on this play, Mallory, we are going to picket the performance. We're going to hand out papers telling everyone it's just one big lie by an untalented nut."

"You would not," I said.

"Oh, yes we would!" cried Adam.

Together, they turned their backs to me and stomped up the aisle.

"That's enough," I heard Kristy tell the kids on the stage. "Take a break." She hopped down off the stage to join me.

"What a mess!" I wailed, flopping into a chair.

Kristy rubbed the back of her neck thoughtfully. "They were pretty ticked off, huh?"

"They're going to picket the play!"

"Why don't you just change their parts? I didn't see all of the play, but from what I did see, it seems a little . . . I don't know . . . a little insulting."

"What about artistic freedom?" I argued.

"Why don't you talk to Ms. Hayes about it?" Kristy suggested.

"Ha!" I laughed scornfully.

"What does that mean?"

"It means Henrietta Hayes won't be any help at all!"

Kristy was confused. "Why not?" she asked.

"Because Henrietta Hayes does *not* write from her own, personal experiences, but *I* do. I won't change my play no matter what!"

"I don't know," Kristy said. "I don't think I agree with you."

"You're entitled to your opinion," I replied stiffly.

I was sure I was right. Only, I thought you were supposed to feel good inside when you did the right thing. So why did I feel so rotten?

CHAPTER 11

The next day, I arrived at Ms. Hayes's house feeling pretty tense. I was angry at her for lying in her books. Still, when she came to the door, my anger melted a bit. Ms. Hayes wasn't someone I could easily be mad at. It's hard to stay mad at your idol.

"Hello, Mallory," she said with a smile. "It's always so good to see you, like a ray of sunshine coming into this shady house." (How could you be mad at someone who said stuff like that?)

Part of me wanted to stay mad, though. Nice as she was, Ms. Hayes was a fake.

"Is something wrong, Mallory?" Ms. Hayes asked.

"Why? What makes you think that?" I asked, probably sounding pretty distressed.

"I don't know, you look rather . . . upset."

"I do?" Why couldn't I just come out and speak my mind? This was certainly the moment to do it. But I couldn't.

I chickened out on the direct approach. Instead, I chose an indirect path. "Ms. Hayes, I need to ask you a few more things to finish up my report. Like, um, what about the Alice Anderson TV movie? What happened to that?"

"It was never made," Ms. Hayes replied. "I didn't like the way they wanted me to change Alice's character, so I backed out of the deal."

That took guts, I thought. Admiring Ms. Hayes's integrity about the TV movie made it even harder to be mad at her.

"Is there anything else you want to know?" Ms. Hayes asked.

"Well, yeah," I replied.

Ms. Hayes checked her watch. "All right. I have about fifteen minutes before George Delmore calls. We're going to talk about the Anderson Family reunion book. Did you come up with any more ideas?"

"Uh, no, not really," I admitted. I'd been too disgusted — and confused — to think about it. But I saw an opening for voicing my complaint. "I mean, I figured, why bother thinking up ideas about the Anderson family? You already know what happened to the Anderson family. Don't you? Their story is your story, isn't it?"

Ms. Hayes frowned. She looked confused

herself. "Of course it's my story, but the reunion book hasn't been written yet."

"Well, maybe not on paper, but you know what happens," I said.

"I have some ideas, yes." Ms. Hayes looked at me as if I'd gone a little crazy. "Why don't we go in the kitchen. You can ask me your questions while we have some hot chocolate."

I nodded and followed Ms. Hayes into her kitchen. "What do you need to know?" she asked, filling her bright blue tea kettle with tap water.

"I need to know more about your family life," I said as I sat at the kitchen table.

Ms. Hayes had turned toward the stove, so I couldn't see her face. Her shoulders tensed, though. Then she relaxed them slightly and turned to face me. "What part of my life?"

"We could start with your childhood. Was your childhood like Alice Anderson's?"

"No," Ms. Hayes replied sadly. "Not at all. I had only one younger brother, but he died in a fire along with my parents. From there I went to many different foster homes. Some were pleasant, others not so pleasant."

"Then I guess Alice Anderson was like your daughter," I said.

"Mallory, I told you, I don't like to talk about my . . . about Cassie," said Ms. Hayes quietly.

"Well, what about Mr. Hayes?" I pressed.

"Hayes is my name. I never changed it. My husband — my ex-husband — is Gregory Rogers, the author. He and I have been divorced for over ten years now."

I pretended to write in my notebook, but I really just scribbled. I knew all this. Why was I asking these cruel questions? Did I want to torture Ms. Hayes or something? "What I'm trying to figure out," I said, "is what part of your life is in the Alice Anderson books."

"What do you mean?" Ms. Hayes asked.

"I mean . . ." I began shakily. I *had* to tell her. I just couldn't hold it in any longer. "I mean you're not being fair to your readers. Your books don't tell anything about your life. They're all made up! They're lies!" By the time I reached the word "lies," my voice was shaking.

Ms. Hayes gave me that blank look I'd seen before. Then she drew her shoulders back, suddenly looking taller. "Mallory," she said in an even, cool voice, "I have not lied. My books are not meant to reflect my life. They are novels. Fiction. I suggest you look up the definition of those words in the dictionary before you go about hurling accusations."

The phone rang then. "Excuse me, that's probably George, calling ahead of schedule,"

Ms. Hayes said in a formal voice.

With a final icy stare, Ms. Hayes went toward her study.

I sat a moment, trying to absorb what she'd said. Was it true? No, it wasn't. I knew what fiction meant. You didn't have to report every fact, as if you were writing a newspaper article, but the heart of your story had to be true.

How could she write about happy families if she didn't know what it was like to be in one? It was as simple as that to me, no matter how she tried to weasel out of it. Yet I liked her books so much! I really did!

This was confusing. And what would it do to my project? It was way too late to change it now. Still, I knew there was only one right thing for me to do.

I tore a piece of paper from my spiral notebook and began to write.

Dear Ms. Hayes,

After today I don't think you will want me to be your assistant anymore. I don't think I could work for you anymore anyway. I'm sorry if I have offended you. You've been very nice to me. It's just that I admired you and your work so much that I thought I could learn something about life and writing from it, and from you. I was *wrong, though. Thank you very much for all your time. I will always appreciate that.*

Sincerely, Mallory

Putting the letter in the middle of the table, I stood up and walked outside. It was beginning to get dark. The trees rustled overhead, sending a light shower of brown and red leaves to the ground. I took my bike from the side of the house and began walking it down the path.

Tears welled in my eyes as I passed the line of trees and neared the road. Wiping them with the sleeves of my jacket, I climbed on my bike and started to ride. As I pedaled, I had the awful feeling that I'd just turned my back on one of the most wonderful people I'd ever known. Stop thinking she's so great, I commanded myself. Henrietta Hayes isn't who you thought she was.

With my head bent against the wind, I pedaled hard up Morgan Road, away from Henrietta Hayes and her happy books of a made-up, fake family, and toward the real-life Pike family — who were mostly not talking to me at all.

CHAPTER 12

I cracked open my bedroom door and peeked out. It was unbelievable! They were still there. My brothers and sisters marched back and forth in front of my room carrying picket signs. "Mallory Pike unfair!" read the one Vanessa held. "The Spikes are a lie!" read Byron's sign. Even Claire had drawn a picture of me in crayon and then drawn a red circle around the picture and slashed a line across it — an international sign for No Mallory. "Mallory-busters!" she chanted as she paced the hallway with the others.

When I'd returned from Ms. Hayes's house that afternoon, the picket line had been in front of the house. "This is just practice!" Vanessa cried as they followed me upstairs. They'd been picketing the hallway for the last hour.

Shutting the door, I shook my head wearily. What a weird family. I didn't know what they were mad about. Judging from the way they were acting now, I'd treated them kindly in my play. They were really a bunch of nuts.

There was a knock on my door and I opened it a crack, half expecting to get a pie in the face or something. But it was Mom. "Can I come in?" she asked.

"Sure," I said, opening the door wider. As Mom stepped in, Margo caught my eye and stuck out her tongue. I wasn't going to stoop to that level, so I just gave her my best icy glare and shut the door.

"Vanessa tells me you wrote a play about our family," said Mom, getting right to the point. I nodded. "She says it's very insulting," Mom added.

"It's not insulting, it's true to life," I defended myself.

"Nicky says his character walks around with a bucket on his head," Mom said. "I've never seen Nicky with a bucket on his head."

"It's just a little comedy bit to dramatize how the boys are always falling or getting hurt or crashing into stuff every two seconds," I explained. "It wouldn't be as interesting if I just had my characters getting hurt all the time the way they really do."

"I see. It's a little artistic license," said Mom.

"What's that?" I asked.

"That's when you change things around a

little to make them more interesting. Strictly speaking, what you've written isn't true."

"But it's basically true," I added.

"The heart of it is true, yes," Mom agreed.

"Then that's what I've done. I've used artistic license."

"Could I read your play?" Mom asked.

"You could," I agreed. "But it would be better if you could see it. I'm going to the elementary school tomorrow for a rehearsal, if you'd like to come."

"All right. That's what I'll do," said Mom. "Aren't you home from Ms. Hayes's house early?"

"Yes. I . . . I don't think I'll be going there anymore. She doesn't really have enough for me to do." I didn't feel like talking about the real reason right then.

Mom studied me. "Did anything happen with Ms. Hayes?"

"No, nothing," I lied.

"All right," said Mom. "Supper will be ready soon."

"Do you mind if I don't eat?" I asked. "I'm not hungry."

Mom smiled. "Are you nervous about eating with the Pike family picketers?"

Truthfully, the idea didn't thrill me. I just wanted to be alone. "They don't bother me," I said. "But I'm not hungry."

"Okay," Mom agreed, but she sounded reluctant.

That night Vanessa came to our room, changed into her pajamas, and went to bed without even looking at me. I had no great desire to look at or speak with her either. Instead, I opened to the last chapter of *Alice Anderson's Greatest Challenge*. I read one sentence and then tossed the book on the floor. Why bother reading a bunch of lies.

After a minute or two, my curiosity won out and I picked the book up again. I needed to know what happened. "Shut off the light, please," Vanessa said snootily. I snapped off the light and went under the covers with my flashlight.

It took me less than an hour to finish the book. Alice Anderson asked for some time off from her role in the movie to go home and take care of her sick mother. It took so long that she called up the director and said she couldn't be in the movie. Then one day the film crew showed up at her house. The director loved Alice's little town, so he stayed and shot other scenes there. Everyone was excited, and Alice was not only on the road to stardom, but the people of her hometown got together and gave her an award for bringing fame and new business to their community.

I have to admit, I was smiling when Alice burst into happy tears over the award. Then I remembered it was written by a fake, and forced myself to stop smiling.

I shut off the flashlight and fell asleep under my covers. I had a terrible dream. I dreamed Pow had a dog collar covered with little spikes. Suddenly, the spikes flew off the collar and started attacking me. I guess you don't have to be a genius psychiatrist to figure out why I dreamed of being attacked by spikes.

In the morning I awoke to a silent Vanessa, and found a note in my cereal bowl on the kitchen table. "Pikes on strike against Spikes," it said.

"What are spikes?" Mom asked, reading the note over my shoulder.

"That's the name of the family in the play."

"Oh, Mal, couldn't you have picked a better name?" Mom asked.

"It rhymes."

"How about the Likes or the Tykes."

"Dumb," I commented.

"Oh," said Mom. "Well, I'll meet you at the elementary school auditorium after school."

"Okay," I agreed, grabbing a handful of Cheerios from the box.

Two handfuls later, I had met Jessi and we were walking to school together. "Mom is coming to rehearsal today," I told her. "Want to come?"

"Sure. But there's something I think you should know. I hate to tell you this, Mal, but Becca told me the play is insulting and that she's not sure if she should be in it."

"What?" I cried.

"Charlotte and Haley might drop out, too," Jessi reported. "They feel they're being disloyal to Vanessa. I told Becca that they couldn't leave you just like that, but they're not the only ones. Nicky told Buddy Barrett he couldn't ever see Pow again if Buddy was in the play."

"Are you kidding?" (We got Pow from the Barretts when Marnie Barrett developed an allergy to animal dander. Buddy and Suzi Barrett are still very attached to Pow and come to visit him often.) "I'll kill Nicky!"

Later that day, when I arrived at the elementary school, I found the Pike picket line in full swing. My darling siblings were marching back and forth in front of the double doors with their idiotic signs. It was mortifying!

"Make them stop," I said to Mom who was standing by the line.

"Mom, you wouldn't cross a picket line, would you?" asked Adam.

115

"Think of me as an impartial arbitrator," said Mom.

"So, you admit you're being a traitor!" shouted Vanessa.

"No," Mom explained. "An arbitrator is someone who tries to find a solution which is fair to both parties in a dispute. Impartial means I'm not on either side. I'm alone in the middle."

"Come on, Mom, I have to start this rehearsal," I said. "Make them go home."

"That's enough, kids," said Mom. "Head home. Stacey and Mary Anne are waiting for you with Claire."

With a lot of grumbling and dirty looks, they shouldered their signs and left. Mom and I went into the auditorium. Jessi was there with the kids, who were already sitting on the edge of the stage. "Hi, Mal. Hi, Mrs. Pike," Jessi greeted us as she hopped off the stage. She hurried up the aisle toward us, looking as if she had something important to say. "Mal, I think I headed off a crisis for you," she said.

"Not another one." I sighed.

"I told Haley, Becca, and Buddy that your mom was here to decide if the play was insulting. If she says it isn't, they'll stay in the play. If she says it *is* insulting, they want out."

"Mom, you have to say it's okay," I pleaded.

"Mallory, I'll give you my honest opinion," Mom insisted as she took a seat in the third row.

Jessi and I herded the kids into their positions on stage. Luckily, Danielle was back. She looked a bit worn, but her dark eyes were shining with excitement. "I memorized all my lines while I waited in the doctor's office," she told me.

"Good work," I said sincerely. "Give this your best. Today is an important rehearsal. The whole future of the play depends on it."

"I'll try," Danielle assured me, and I knew she would.

"Okay, everybody, take it from the top!" I yelled as I went back to my seat in the front row next to Jessi.

Danielle came out and said her first line. "How I wish I could write something truly great . . ."

I glanced at Mom. She smiled back at me. I figured that was a good sign.

Next, Haley came in as Jill, the Vanessa part which I'd rewritten. She still held her script since the lines were new. "Valery, Valery, what could it be? Why am I not more like thee? With wit so quick, and heart so kind, surpassed by only your brilliant mind. What do you think of my latest poem, Valery?"

Danielle as Valery replied with new lines I'd

given her character. "It's lovely, Jill. But you have to stop comparing yourself to me. You're your own person with your own unique talents."

I sneaked another peek at Mom. She had to have liked that line. This time she didn't notice me. She sat forward with her chin propped on her fingertips, watching the play intently.

"Oh, Valery, I don't know how you put up with the rest of us," said Haley as Jill. Then Haley put her hands on her hips and took two strides to the front of the stage. "Vanessa would never say something like that," she objected. "Never in a billion years."

"Just say the lines the way they're written," I told her impatiently.

Buddy came spinning onstage with a real bucket — in which he'd cut two eye holes — over his head. "Help! Help! I'm stuck!" he cried.

I almost jumped up to object to the eyeholes, but I thought that it might be best not to call too much attention to the bucket. In the new version, Jill pulled the bucket off but didn't fall down. She said, "On his head he wears a pail unintentionally stuck. Oh, Valery how can you stand to live with such a cluck?"

"Jill, please stop rhyming," said Danielle as Valery. "It gets a little annoying after awhile."

"Sorry, Valery," Jill (Haley) replied. "Sometimes I just can't stop myself."

Wendy came on, twirling the Skip-It over her head. The Skip-It slipped from her hands and bonked Haley on the head.

"Ow! Watch it!" Haley cried.

"That wasn't supposed to happen," I told Mom.

Mom nodded slowly. I didn't like the pained expression on her face. And the play had just begun. By the time Char came on as Mom and asked Valery to do all that work, I had a pretty strong feeling that the arbitrator's verdict might not go in my favor. I checked Mom's expression, and saw that her eyebrows were arched and her lips were tight — not a good sign at all.

"Good job," I told the kids when the play was done. "We'll meet again on Monday. I want everyone to have all their lines memorized by then."

"Wait a minute," Char objected. "We want to hear what your mother has to say first."

I turned to Mom. "What did you think?" I asked nervously.

"It's pretty insulting, Mal," she said softly.

"She didn't like it, did she?" cried Char. "I told you," she said to Becca.

"Mallory, I have to quit," Buddy spoke up. "I'm sorry, but I have to."

"Me too," said Haley.

"We do too," Char and Becca spoke up together.

"Mom! Say something to them!" I begged. "It wasn't *that* bad!"

"What about a rewrite?" Mom suggested. "You could soften the characters."

"But the play will be performed in a week. They can't learn a new play in that amount of time," I objected.

"They don't all know their lines now," Jessi reminded me. "It shouldn't make that much difference."

"But I don't want to write an untrue play," I said to Mom. "I don't want to tell lies the way . . . the way . . . some authors do."

"This isn't a true picture as it is now, Mal," Mom insisted. "Your brothers and sisters all have endearing traits as well as annoying characteristics, just as all people do. Just as you do."

"Sorry about having to quit, Mallory," said Charlotte as she climbed down off the stage.

"Hold on," I told her and the rest of the cast. "All right. I'll do some rewriting. Would you all agree to wait until you see the revision?"

The kids looked at one another.

"The revision will probably make it okay," Jessi said to the kids. "Why don't you give Mallory a break?"

"I don't want Nicky mad at me," said Buddy.

"Buddy, you can see Pow no matter what," I told him. "But I promise, my brothers and sisters will approve of the next script. I'll have them initial it if it will make you happy."

"That would be good," said Becca.

"All right," I said.

What had I done? I was letting others tell me what I should write. Then again, Mom had said it wasn't true the way it was. *I* thought it was. But if no one else agreed, how true could it be?

My head began to swim. Not only would I have to rethink the essay part of my project about Ms. Hayes, I had to rethink my play now, too.

CHAPTER 13

"I'm not initialing this," Margo told me on Thursday afternoon. By working like crazy, I'd finished revising my play. It wasn't exactly the play I'd set out to write, since it wasn't as true to life, but it was still pretty good.

"Why won't you sign?" I asked Margo. "What's wrong with this play?"

"My character is named Muriel now. I hate that name. When you rewrote the play, you gave everybody else good names."

"Margo," I snapped impatiently. "What name would you like?"

"Melissa," she said. "It's the name Mom and Dad should have named me. I'm definitely a Melissa."

I flipped open my manuscript, crossed out "Muriel," and printed in "Melissa." "There, Margo, you are now Melissa. Happy?"

Margo smiled and nodded as she initialed the play. Hers was the last signature I needed.

All the rest of my brothers and sisters had read the play (Claire had had it read to her) and said it was all right by them. Mom had made a copy of it and was reading it that very moment.

Now everything depended on the Kids Club. They'd only have two more rehearsals before I had to show Mr. Williams a production of the play. They'd have to memorize a lot of new lines in a very short time.

They weren't the only ones who would be busy between now and the play. The elementary school auditorium would only be available to me next Wednesday, so that's when I'd have to do the play. But my report was due in four days, by Monday. I had to get going on it tonight.

But how could I compare the way my life influenced my work and the way Ms. Hayes's life influenced hers, when my play had been changed because it was so unpopular, and Ms. Hayes's writing wasn't based on her life at all?

As I do whenever I have a big problem, I called Jessi. She answered the phone and I explained my problem to her. "Any ideas?" I asked hopefully.

"Well," she began, "it seems sort of like a science experiment."

"What do you mean?"

"In a science experiment you set out to test something, a hypothesis, but if your result isn't what you thought it would be, then that's your answer."

"I still don't get it," I admitted.

"Sometimes in an experiment you get an answer you never expected. That doesn't mean your experiment was a failure. It could mean you were asking the wrong question. It could mean you learned something new, and your experiment was even more valuable than if you'd gotten the result you expected. You know, that's how scientists discover new things."

"Thanks, I think," I told her. "How's your project coming?"

"All right, I guess. I was typing up the story of *The Nutcracker* when you called. Mr. Williams wanted me to illustrate my stories, too. That's going to be the hard part for me."

"Good luck," I said. "I'm going to hang up now and think some more about what you said. I understand what you mean, but I'm not exactly sure what I *did* learn from all this."

"Okay, see you tomorrow," said Jessi.

Back in my room I sat at my desk and stared at the blank pages in front of me. What *had* I learned?

There was a rap on the door and Mom came

in. She held the play in her hand. "This version is much better," she told me as she handed it to me.

"Do you really think so?"

"I think it's a much better play than it was," Mom said. "It's funnier and more touching. It seems like your writing improved when you paid more attention to writing a good play and a bit less attention to trying to show an accurate portrayal of our family. I think it's now a very good play."

"Thanks," I said thoughtfully.

Mom smiled and patted my shoulder. After she left, I went back to staring at the blank paper in front of me. In a moment I started writing.

I began this project with the idea that an author must write about her or his life experience. I thought it was the only way to be a good writer. But now I'm not sure this is really as true as I'd thought.

I wrote honestly about my experiences with *The Early Years*. As I wrote, I came to see more clearly how I'd concentrated too narrowly on my family life. In writing my second version, I tried to write an interesting story with interesting and realistic characters. When I did that, the entire picture changed. And the second play was better.

Then I came to the compare and contrast part. What about Henrietta Hayes? Had she had any experience from which the truth of a happy family could have come? Now that I thought about it, I hadn't given her a chance to tell me. I'd been kind of harsh, really. I probably owed her the chance to tell me what she'd been thinking. After all, I'd been given another chance by the people who didn't think I'd told the truth in *my* writing.

Glancing out the window, I saw that although it was late afternoon, there was an hour or so of daylight left. I could probably make it to Ms. Hayes's house and back before dark.

I picked my jacket up off the bed, and headed out of the house. As I pedaled my bike toward Morgan Road, I wondered if Ms. Hayes was angry at me. Would she even want to talk to me? Why should she? But I felt as though I had to try, so I kept on going.

I reached her house, and walked my bike through the trees. Approaching her door, I felt as nervous as I had the very first day I'd come there.

I knocked on the door, and Ms. Hayes answered quickly. "Mallory," she greeted me, obviously surprised to see me. "Come in."

Luckily, there was warmth in her voice and a welcoming look on her face. If she'd been cold I might have bolted out of there, too nervous to go on. "Ms. Hayes, I'm sorry for the way I ran out last week," I apologized sincerely.

She nodded, that blank look coming over her face. I realized that was her thinking look. What was she thinking now? "I'm very glad you're here," Ms. Hayes said. "Sit down, and we can talk."

I took a seat on the couch. Ms. Hayes sat in a large cushiony chair by the end of the couch. "I intended to write you a letter," she said. "A real letter," she added with a quick smile, "because I've given a great deal of thought to what you said the other day. You know, in some ways, I think you're right."

"You do?"

"And in many ways I think you're wrong. Mallory, you know a story doesn't have to be autobiographical. It's a story that you, as an author, make up. It can be the story of someone else's life, or a story of your own fantasy. Yet, here's where I think you're correct. What you write *should* tell things that you honestly know to be true of the world. And I have tried to always do that in my books. You've enjoyed my books, haven't you?"

"I *love* your books!" I said sincerely.

"I think you responded so well to them because you sensed the emotional truth in the stories."

"That makes sense," I agreed.

"Good writing has more to do with perfecting your artistry as a storyteller and sharpening your skill with words than it has to do with the raw material of your life."

"But did you know someone like Alice Anderson?" I asked.

"Yes, I did," said Ms. Hayes. "When I was eleven I spent a year with a foster family on a small farm in upstate New York. Their names were the Larsons, but they became the Andersons in my books. Alice was modelled on Linda Larson. She was a wonderful girl, and her brothers were wonderful, too. I wished I could have stayed there and lived with them forever, but that's not how the foster care system works."

"So what you wrote *was* true. I'm so sorry," I said, feeling like an idiot.

"I didn't write about them exactly as they were," Ms. Hayes said. "They had their problems and their human failings, as all of us do. But they still seemed like a very happy family. With all their problems, I would have chosen to belong to that family rather than be all alone, the way I was."

"So their story is almost true," I said, still trying to understand.

"There's a great deal of truth in it," Ms. Hayes said. "I wrote the first Alice Anderson book right after Cassie died and — "

"You don't have to talk about it," I interrupted.

"It's all right. I will this once. Cassie and I never got along smoothly. During her last two years in high school we argued a lot." Ms. Hayes took off her thick glasses and wiped tears from her red-rimmed eyes. "The last time I saw Cassie alive we were exchanging bitter words. I'll have to live with that forever."

"That must be hard for you," I said, imagining — or trying to imagine — how awful she must feel.

"It *was* hard."

Ms. Hayes smiled a little sadly. "You know, Mallory, talking to you has gotten me thinking about my childhood. Maybe I *will* write a book about my childhood — a nonfiction book. But, before I think about that, I need to finish *The Anderson Family Reunion*. I have to submit a final outline to George in two days. Are you still interested in helping?"

"I'd love to," I said. "I'll have to call home and ask if I can stay after dark."

"Naturally, I'll call a cab to take you home."

I called and Dad said it would be all right. I really should have spent the evening working on my project, but after all the help Ms. Hayes had given me, how could I refuse to help her? Besides, this was something I really wanted to do.

CHAPTER 14

"This is excellent work, Mallory, really excellent," Mr. Williams said to me in front of the whole class on the following Wednesday. He'd read our projects over the past two nights. Mine was the last one he returned.

"Thank you," I said. "But that's only half of it."

"I know that," Mr. Williams said. "I'll be in the auditorium this afternoon to see your play, and then I'll grade the entire project."

Jessi caught my eye and gave me an enthusiastic thumbs-up.

"Anyone who'd like to see Mallory's first play is welcome to go to the elementary school auditorium after school," Mr. Williams told the class.

I was already nervous about the play. The thought of the entire class showing up made me even more nervous. Our final rehearsal, just yesterday, had been spotty —

some parts smooth, some parts not-so-smooth. There were a lot of forgotten lines because of the script changes. I'd just have to keep my fingers crossed and hope for the best. I really wanted it to be good. Besides the fact that my grade depended on it, I'd invited Ms. Hayes to come see my play.

When I arrived at the elementary school that afternoon, I spotted my friends from the BSC. "How long is this play?" Kristy asked me, checking her watch.

"Don't worry," I said. "It's not more than an hour. We'll be done in plenty of time for our meeting."

"Good."

Mary Anne smiled and rolled her eyes at Kristy. "Good luck with the play," she said to me.

"You changed it, didn't you?" Stacey asked anxiously.

"Yes. My brothers and sisters think it's all right now," I told her.

"Oh, yeah? Are you sure about that?" Claudia asked skeptically. She was looking at something over my shoulder, so I turned to see what it was.

"Oh, no!" I groaned. My brothers and sisters were arriving — in disguise! Byron, Adam, and Jordan each wore one of those crazy-looking nose and mustache things attached to black-rimmed glasses. Vanessa had on dark sunglasses and a too-big man's fedora. Margo had on a scarf and dark glasses. Nicky wore a ski mask. They'd even brought Claire along. She was wearing her Minnie Mouse mask from Halloween.

"Very funny, you guys," I said when they neared the front doors. "Take that stuff off, would you?"

"No way," Vanessa insisted. "We're not taking any chances."

"Everyone will laugh at you for sure if you wear those disguises inside," I argued.

"We'd rather be laughed at for *looking* weird than for *being* weird," said Jordan.

"You read the play. You're not weird anymore," I reminded them.

"Maybe that copy was just to show us. Maybe you're putting on the old one," Vanessa said. "Come on," she told the others. They followed her into the auditorium.

"Oh, no, they're not weird," I said sarcastically. "Not at all. They're *totally* normal."

Everyone laughed. "Don't you have to go inside and make sure your actors are ready?" Stacey asked.

"Right. I should," I agreed. "Jessi's probably already in there. See you later."

I ran down the aisle and into the backstage entrance, off to the right side of the stage.

"We're all set," said Jessi, who was helping me along with Ms. Simon.

"Great. Thanks," I said. "Come here, everyone." The kids gathered around me, dressed in their neatest clothes. Danielle wore a bright red corduroy jumper with a white blouse underneath. On her head she wore a thin red scarf, tied in the back, with a slouchy red corduroy hat over it. She looked pretty, despite the faint circles under her eyes.

"Do you all know your lines?" I asked. The group nodded, but I noticed some uncertain expressions. On Tuesday, Tony still hadn't known his part very well. I prayed he'd spent the night studying Ed's lines. (Nicky had insisted his character's name be changed to Ed. For some reason, he'd decided Ed was "the coolest name a guy could have.")

"All right, everybody, do your best and good luck," said Ms. Simon as she hurried by. "Do you think they're set?" she whispered to me.

"I hope so," I replied with my fingers crossed.

Jessi had gone to peek out the curtain. "I see a woman I don't recognize. From your description I think she might be Ms. Hayes," she reported in a whisper. "Your mother is here, and your father is with her."

"Dad?" I exclaimed, peeking out. "Wow! He

must have left work early just for this."

"There's Aunt Cecelia and Squirt," Jessi added. "And there's Dr. Johanssen. And Mrs. Barrett with Marnie and Suzi."

Looking over her shoulder, I saw them walking in with other family members, including Mrs. Braddock and Haley's brother Matt. "If I'd known Matt was coming I'd have arranged for someone to sign for him," I said. (Matt Braddock is profoundly deaf.)

"Mrs. Braddock will sign for him," Jessi reminded me.

"That's true."

"It's almost curtain time," said Ms. Simon. "Better get set."

"All right," I said.

Jessi and I brought out the cot which would be Valery's bed and the folding chair that went next to it. "Curtain going up!" I told my cast, which wasn't exactly accurate since our curtain pulled to either side, not up. It sounded better than "curtain to the side," though.

Jessi and I pulled on the curtain as Ms. Simon walked to the center of the stage. "Welcome, everyone," she said to the audience. "Today you are here to see a new play by a bright young playwright. It's about the struggles of a young person to find herself as a writer while still being a loving member of a happy and very active family. We hope you enjoy *The Early Years*, written by Ms. Mallory Pike and performed by members of the Kids Can Do Anything Club."

Everyone clapped. Ms. Simon left the stage and Danielle walked on. She spoke her first line: "How I wish I could write something truly great, something that would change the world and make people happy, especially children."

I noticed Haley off to the side, staring into space. "That's your cue to enter," I whispered urgently to her.

"I'm scared," she whispered back.

I glanced nervously at Danielle. "A rare moment of quiet," she ad-libbed, killing time until Haley showed up. "I think I'll begin writing something now. But what? That's the hard problem."

Good work, Danielle, I thought. "Go, Haley, please," I begged. "Your mother and brother are out there."

"They are?" Haley asked. "I didn't see them come in."

"I did."

Taking a deep breath, Haley stepped onto the stage. "Hi, Valery," she said. "Are you writing again?"

The response was supposed to be, "No, I haven't started." Danielle changed it to, "Yes,

I just started," to fit in with her own improvised lines.

"I don't want to interrupt you, but I was hoping for your opinion of my latest poem," said Haley as Jill.

"Sure, go ahead," Danielle, as Valery, replied.

I put one of Vanessa's real poems in here, a nice one. Haley read it. "That's terrific," said Danielle.

"Thanks," replied Haley.

Jessi gave Tony a gentle push onto the stage after he missed his cue. "Hi, you guys," ran his new opening line. "Has anyone seen Zow's leash?" (I'd even given Pow a fictionalized name, although he was the only member of my family who hadn't bothered me about his character.)

"I think it's in your room," said Danielle.

"No, it's in the front hall closet," said Haley.

"Thanks, Mallory. Thanks, Vanessa," Tony said, leaving. "Um, I mean, Valery and Ranessa. No, Jill! Thanks, Jill and Mallory. I mean, Valery . . . or whatever it is."

Again, Danielle covered. "That Ed, he's such a joker — always pretending he doesn't know anyone's name."

"Yes, he's always playing jokes like that," Haley joined in.

Next Wendy came on as Melissa, skipping

rope. "I jumped all the way to one hundred," she said. "Does anyone want to see me do it?"

"Valery needs to write, Melissa," said Haley.

"It's all right," said Danielle. "Let's see, Melissa."

While Wendy jumped and Haley counted, Becca entered, as the Jessi character. "Hi, Sissy," Danielle said.

"Hi," said Becca. "Did you get your writing done?"

"No," Danielle replied. "I've had a few . . . um . . . interruptions."

"I don't know how you write anything in this house," said Wendy.

Charlotte, as my mother, came on. "Val, I hate to ask you this," she said in a tiny voice I'm sure no one could hear, "but could you watch the kids with Sissy while I run to the store for milk? I'll be right back."

"Sure, Mom," said Danielle. When Char left, Danielle threw her arms into the air and made a funny face. "It's nearly impossible to write anything when you're a member of the busy Turnpike family."

That was the cue for Buddy, Peter, and Bruce to walk on as the triplets (now named Mike, John, and Bob). Each of them was dribbling a basketball. Then Sara Hill came in as

Delaware. (Claire liked that name.) Dressed in a tutu, she danced around the stage.

"See what I mean?" Danielle asked Becca. "Being a Turnpike is like *living* on the turnpike — in heavy traffic."

"I see what you mean," Becca replied. Both girls made comical faces. The audience laughed, which made me happy because I hoped they would laugh right there.

The rest of the play went pretty smoothly. There were a few little problems (such as when the cot collapsed in the middle of Valery's sick scene) and some mix-ups (such as when Buddy Barrett walked on in the middle of the wrong scene). Mostly, though, I'd say it was a success.

At the end, everyone came out for a curtain call. The audience clapped loudly. When Danielle stepped forward, they cheered, and rose to their feet for a standing ovation. She really deserved it, too. She'd been great.

Then someone started shouting, "Author! Author!" The audience took up the chant.

"Go on," said Jessi. "Go out there."

I walked onstage. The cast clapped for me and I looked out into the audience and saw everyone still standing. Ms. Hayes was right up front, smiling away. My parents looked pretty proud, too. My brothers and sisters were standing along with everybody else.

They'd even taken off their disguises.

I didn't realize how hard I was smiling until I noticed that my cheeks hurt. Mr. Katz walked onstage holding four red roses. He handed two to Danielle, which started everyone cheering all over again. He handed the second two to me. I knew there was someone else who deserved a rose as much as I did. I walked to the edge of the stage and reached down, handing one of my roses to Henrietta Hayes.

CHAPTER 15

I felt like a celebrity. After the final curtain went down everyone congratulated me and shook my hand and patted my back. It was the greatest feeling. "A definite A-plus," Mr. Williams said when he came backstage. "Between us, it was by far the best project in the class."

"Thanks," I said, smiling from ear to ear. "I can't believe how much I learned."

"That was the idea," said Mr. Williams as he left.

Ms. Simon and Mr. Katz came over to me next, surrounded by my Kids Club cast. "We have a request," said Ms. Simon.

"Anything," I said. "I owe you guys a lot. You helped me land an A-plus on my project."

"The kids would like you to write an updated, kids' version of *A Christmas Carol* for them to perform at the pediatric ward of the hospital over the holidays," Mr. Katz told me.

"Like, Scrooge is the big bully in the school-yard," said Haley. "And these kid ghosts come and visit him one night."

"What a cool idea," I said excitedly. "I'll start working on it right away."

"Danielle should be Scrooge," suggested Haley, "since she's our star."

Danielle smiled. "I wouldn't mind."

The kids went their own ways as their parents came back to congratulate them. Mrs. Ramsey came over to me with Squirt squirming in her arms. "We really enjoyed the play, Mal," she said.

"Thank you," I replied. "Becca did a great job playing Jessi, or I should say, Sissy."

Becca and Jessi came over with their arms around one another. Jessi put her other arm around me. "I'm surrounded by talent," she said. "Lucky me."

My family came backstage next. "Nice job, Mal," said Dad.

"It was wonderful," Mom agreed.

"Pretty cool," Byron said.

"Haley did a good job reading my poem," said Vanessa. "Do you think the people liked it?"

"I'm sure they did," I told her. "It's a good poem."

Standing by the door, I noticed Ms. Hayes. She still held the rose I'd given her. "I'll be right back," I told my family.

"I am so proud of you, Mallory," Ms. Hayes said when I joined her. "That was a terrific first play."

"It went through a few rewrites," I admitted.

"Most good work does," Ms. Hayes said. She fished in her large black leather shoulder bag and pulled out a stack of papers held together with a red rubber band. "Here's an outline, for example, which went through several revisions." She handed it to me. "This is the outline and the first three chapters of *The Anderson Family Reunion*. Look at the acknowledgements page, the tenth or eleventh page, I believe."

I thumbed through to the eleventh page. When I read it, I looked up, wide-eyed with amazement. "Ms. Hayes," I gasped. "You put my name on this."

It said: The author thanks Mallory Pike for suggesting the idea for this book and for her valuable input.

"The book was your idea, and many of your ideas are in here. You deserve the credit," said Ms. Hayes.

"Oh, but I never expected . . . I . . . This is so great. Thank you!"

"You're very welcome, Mallory," said Ms. Hayes. "You certainly deserve it. This is a copy for you. I sent another copy off to George Delmore this morning."

Filled with happiness, pride, and gratitude, I threw my arms around Ms. Hayes. I always knew someday I'd see my name in a book, but I never expected it to be so soon.

My parents came over and introduced themselves. "You have a very special, talented girl here," said Ms. Hayes. "I'm sure you know that."

"Yes, we do," said Dad.

"But thank you for saying so," added Mom politely.

Ms. Hayes said good-bye and turned to leave. "Will I see you next Tuesday?" she asked me.

"Absolutely," I said. "Don't file a thing until I get there."

Ms. Hayes laughed, and, with a wave, went off down the hall. "What a nice woman," said Mom.

"She's great," I agreed, handing Mom the manuscript. "Look at this."

My parents were very impressed. "I think this calls for a celebration," said Mom. "Why don't you invite your friends over. I'll order pizzas."

"Great!" I said. I didn't have to look far for my friends. They were just walking in.

"Mallory! Mallory!" they chanted.

"Way to go!" said Claudia, slapping me five.

"Excellent job," said Kristy.

After my friends had congratulated me, I invited them to the pizza party. "Sounds like fun," said Claudia. "I'll be there." The others said they could make it, too.

Then Kristy checked her watch. "It's five o'clock," she announced.

We all knew what that meant.

"Let's go," I said. "Hey, maybe Dad can give us a ride."

Looking around, I saw that my family had left, but I thought I might still be able to catch up with them if they'd gone back out to the auditorium. I took a shortcut across the stage and found Mom and Dad standing in the aisle talking to Mrs. Barrett.

"Sure, I can fit everyone in," Dad agreed, when I asked him to drive us to Claudia's house. "I'll meet you in the parking lot."

Hopping back on the stage, I crossed to the wings. Out in the auditorium, and behind me, backstage, people chattered noisily. But there in the darkened stage wings it was almost quiet.

I looked out across the shiny floor of the stage and thought about everything that had happened. Even though I was still the same age, I felt older, as if the kid part of my life had somehow ended, and another part had just begun. It was an exciting feeling — scary, but also thrilling. Who knew what big changes were up ahead, waiting for me?

"It's five after five," reported Kristy from behind me.

"Okay," I said. "My dad will give us a ride."

As my friends and I walked to the car, I thought about how Ms. Hayes had found inspiration for the Alice Anderson books in the happiest time of her life. If I were to write about the happiest time of my life, what would I pick?

I didn't think about it for more than a moment.

The first sentences of that book sprang to my head.

Valery Turnpike produced her first play, saw her work with a famous author completed, and was surrounded by good friends and family all on the same day. Valery tended to be a complainer, but on that day she opened her eyes and realized for the first time that she was a very, very lucky person.

About the Author

ANN M. MARTIN did *a lot* of baby-sitting when she was growing up in Princeton, New Jersey. She is a former editor of books for children, and was graduated from Smith College.

Ms. Martin lives in New York City with her cats, Mouse and Rosie. She likes ice cream and *I Love Lucy*; and she hates to cook.

Ann Martin's Apple Paperbacks include *Yours Turly, Shirley*; *Ten Kids, No Pets*; *With You and Without You*; *Bummer Summer*; and all the other books in the Baby-sitters Club series.

Look for #81

KRISTY AND MR. MOM

"First of all, I'd like to compliment the chef."
Watson raised his glass to Nannie and we followed suit.

"To the chef!"

"Now, I'd like to tell you, my wonderful family, how much you mean to me and just how happy I am to be able to stand here and look at your beaming faces." He raised his glass to the family. "Here's looking at you, kids!"

"To us!" we cried, gleefully.

David Michael took that as his cue. "I'd like to propose a toast to Shannon, Boo-Boo, Goldfishie, and Crystal Light the second."

Watson grinned and raised his glass. "To the Brewer Zoo."

"To the zoo!" we chorused.

Mom stood up. "Now I'd like to make a toast. Welcome home, Watson."

"Hooray for Watson!" David Michael led the cheering.

Emily Michelle loved that. She stood on her chair and clapped her hands together. "Hooway for me! Hooway for me!"

Watson and the rest of us lifted our water glasses to Emily Michelle. "To Emily."

Then Watson cleared his throat. "I made an important decision today that will affect all of us."

"We're not moving, are we?" David Michael suddenly paled. "I have to do my play. The rooster is a really important part."

Watson chuckled. "Don't worry, we're not moving. I like it here. In fact, I like it so much that I've decided to stay home."

"Permanently?" I blinked in surprise. "You mean, quit your job?"

"Not exactly," Watson explained. "I would just turn the business over to one of my vice-presidents at Unity. They can manage the day-to-day affairs and, if they need an executive decision, they can contact me here. But for now, I want to be a stay-at-home dad."

"Mr. Mom," I whispered to Charlie.

Watson heard me and chuckled. "Mr. Mom. Exactly."

Read all the books
about Mallory
in the **Baby-sitters Club** series
by Ann M. Martin

Ann Martin wants *YOU*
to help name the new baby-sitter...and her twin.

Dear Diary,
I'm 13 now...finally
in the 8th grade. My
twin sister and I just
moved here and this
great group of girls
asked me to join their
baby-sitting club...

Name the twins
and win a

THE BABY-SITTERS CLUB

book
dedication!

Simply dream up the first and last names of the new baby-sitter and her twin sister (who's not in the BSC), and fill in the names on the coupon below. One lucky entry will be selected by Ann M. Martin and Scholastic Inc. The winning names will continue to be featured in the series starting next fall 1995, and the winner will have a future BSC book dedicated to her/him!

THE BSC NAME THE TWINS CONTEST

Name the new twins! (First and last, please)

_____ **and** _____

Name _____   Birthdate _____
M / D / Y

Street _____ City _____ State/Zip _____

BSCC1194

THE BABY-SITTERS CLUB®

by Ann M. Martin

More titles... ▶

The Baby-sitters Club titles continued...

❏ MG45659-8	#58 Stacey's Choice	$3.50
❏ MG45660-1	#59 Mallory Hates Boys (and Gym)	$3.50
❏ MG45662-8	#60 Mary Anne's Makeover	$3.50
❏ MG45663-6	#61 Jessi's and the Awful Secret	$3.50
❏ MG45664-4	#62 Kristy and the Worst Kid Ever	$3.50
❏ MG45665-2	#63 Claudia's ~~Freind~~ Friend	$3.50
❏ MG45666-0	#64 Dawn's Family Feud	$3.50
❏ MG45667-9	#65 Stacey's Big Crush	$3.50
❏ MG47004-3	#66 Maid Mary Anne	$3.50
❏ MG47005-1	#67 Dawn's Big Move	$3.50
❏ MG47006-X	#68 Jessi and the Bad Baby-Sitter	$3.50
❏ MG47007-8	#69 Get Well Soon, Mallory!	$3.50
❏ MG47008-6	#70 Stacey and the Cheerleaders	$3.50
❏ MG47009-4	#71 Claudia and the Perfect Boy	$3.50
❏ MG47010-8	#72 Dawn and the We Love Kids Club	$3.50
❏ MG45575-3	Logan's Story Special Edition Readers' Request	$3.25
❏ MG47118-X	Logan Bruno, Boy Baby-sitter Special Edition Readers' Request	$3.50
❏ MG44240-6	Baby-sitters on Board! Super Special #1	$3.95
❏ MG44239-2	Baby-sitters' Summer Vacation Super Special #2	$3.95
❏ MG43973-1	Baby-sitters' Winter Vacation Super Special #3	$3.95
❏ MG42493-9	Baby-sitters' Island Adventure Super Special #4	$3.95
❏ MG43575-2	California Girls! Super Special #5	$3.95
❏ MG43576-0	New York, New York! Super Special #6	$3.95
❏ MG44963-X	Snowbound Super Special #7	$3.95
❏ MG44962-X	Baby-sitters at Shadow Lake Super Special #8	$3.95
❏ MG45661-X	Starring the Baby-sitters Club Super Special #9	$3.95
❏ MG45674-1	Sea City, Here We Come! Super Special #10	$3.95

Available wherever you buy books...or use this order form.

Scholastic Inc., P.O. Box 7502, 2931 E. McCarty Street, Jefferson City, MO 65102

Please send me the books I have checked above. I am enclosing $_____
(please add $2.00 to cover shipping and handling). Send check or money order - no cash or C.O.D.s please.

Name _____ Birthdate_____

Address _____

City_____ State/Zip _____
Please allow four to six weeks for delivery. Offer good in the U.S. only. Sorry, mail orders are not available to residents of Canada. Prices subject to change.

THE BABY-SITTERS CLUB®

Stacey
Claudia
Kristy
Mallory
Dawn
Mary Anne
Jessi

Wow! It's really them-
the new Baby-sitters Club dolls!

Your favorite Baby-sitters Club characters have come to life in these
beautiful collector dolls. Each doll wears her own unique clothes and jewelry.
They look just like the girls you have imagined! The dolls also come with their own
individual stories in special edition booklets that you'll find nowhere else.

Look for the new Baby-sitters Club collection...
coming soon to a store near you!

Kenner®